*For my parents, Lawrence M. Tangvik and
Catherine Eileen Mulligan*

Contents

ACKNOWLEDGEMENTS

I want to acknowledge the following people who are most dear to me for providing inspiration and for exchanging crazy stories over the years: My wife Rose, my kids Marc, Soli, Carol, and Cati; my sisters: Laurene Powers, Bucky Tangvik, and Joyce Fowler; all of the Mulligans, and the Humarock crowd; my blood brothers: Claudio Martinez, Jesús Gerena, Ross Bluestein, Pat Walker, and Luis Fernandez; the fun-loving Charlestown Townies; everyone at the Hyde Square Task Force, especially Brenda Rodriguez-Andujar, Yi-Chin Chen, Chrismaldi Vasquez, Carla Poulos, Enoes Andujar, Nelson Arroyo, Damaris Pimentel and Paul Trunnell.

Thanks to: Friend and colleague David Updike for encouraging me to produce these stories, Carol Gaskins at Editorial Alchemy for her superb editing skills and Ross Murphy at Aberdeen Bay Publishers for believing in this collection.

My appreciation goes to the wise and gifted folks who created and maintain Our Lady of Perpetual Help Basilica in Mission Hill.

Finally, thanks to the thousands of students at Roxbury Community College and at the Hyde Square Task Force who have infinitely enriched my life.

Foreword

Sometime between the 2000 and 2010 Census, Boston officially became a "minority majority" city. In other words, people who check off "white" or "Caucasian" on demographic forms now constitute less than fifty percent of the population. Recent waves of immigrants from the Caribbean, Central and South America, Africa, and Southeast Asia have crashed onto Boston's shores, and channeled their way up Cummings Highway, down Columbia Road, across Bennington Street, through Brighton Ave., and deeply into Tremont Street.

This dynamic dosage of pepper, cinnamon, and curry challenges the reputation Boston earned in the 1970's as a white-dominated, hostile, parochial city of racists. Those internationally broadcasted images of chain-smoking, pit-bull-like white mothers throwing rocks at black kids during school desegregation do not die easily.

In the Zen of Boston, everything stays the same, yet everything changes. Some uglier elements of Beantown's culture remain as stubborn as the rats in the Fens. Blacks and whites still don't trust each other, never mind hang out. Drive-by suburban junkies help keep the street drug trade alive. The major business, media and political leaders remain overwhelmingly white and oblivious to the exploding Latino population. Our public high schools are locked into an apartheid system and nobody has a key. It is rare that a black man enters a downtown jewelry store with arousing suspicions. Cranky whites bark "SPEAK ENGLISH" to timid-looking female immigrants in the streets, buses, trains and stores. Very few black folks enjoy Fenway Park. Suburban drivers who get lost and end up on Blue Hill Ave. nervously lock their doors, fearing a car jacking. No, *The Hub* has never exuded the more open, cosmopolitan, multi-cultural ambiance of our upscale cousin, *The Big Apple*.

But a peek into the barrios reveals tones of change. Young black females with attitude are challenging racial profiling in retail stores. Dominicans, after taking over the public housing projects in the Irish strongholds of Charlestown and South Boston, have also claimed the Pulitzer Prize. Mixed-race couples are getting under the sheets, spawning a whole new generation of "other". Speaking Haitian Creole has now become a requirement for driving a Boston Public School bus. Puerto Ricans are buying brown rice at Whole Foods and carrying yoga mats. Immigrants send millions of hard earned dollars home, creating a massive people-to-people economic aid program. Dollar stores are popping up like dandelions across Hyde Park and Roslindale. White yuppies are dropping up to $100,000 extra for a condo in a "diverse" neighborhood, but then complain about the loud Bachata music. Colombians are renting VFW halls to dance Cumbia on frigid February weekends. There are more Vietnamese restaurants than Irish pubs on Dot Avenue. Gay couples share flower gardening tips with their Irish widowed neighbors in South Boston. Moslems now have the political clout to build a gorgeous mosque on city-controlled property. Brazilians are making more money than anyone by working a hundred hours a week serving donuts, cleaning houses, and renovating apartment buildings. Jamaicans are throwing Super Bowl parties. Nigerians are working the streets as political liaisons to the Mayor, and Guatemalans are playing hockey. Zumba fever (which by the way, could save us all) is breaking out in every corner of the city. And in the midst of all the madness, King Tom and Queen Giselle are uniting the North and South American continents in a Back Bay condo.

So Boston is changing and as the city scratches out its new identity, the masses rise out of bed early each morning with an abundance of fight for three fundamental desires: love, respect, and happiness for our children. And in this struggle, the paths of whites, African-Americans, and the multitudes of immigrants cross in many dimensions. Crashing and clashing, we confound each other, we argue, we trash talk and we send each other to hell. But more and more, we cross boundaries to share laughs, insights and empathetic embraces.

Boston, like much of urban America, is at a critical and exciting time in our rich history. What follows are some loosely-connected stories that have emerged as I have observed, participated in, and imagined a new Bostonian culture taking shape. It is my hope that these stories can sharpen the understanding of our differences and illuminate the common flame of our humanity.

Mariposa

Jazmin hesitated just outside of the subway station, coffee cup in hand, backpack on her denim shoulders. The air still held a chill at 6:55 AM, but the frigid, biting winds that had blistered cheeks and stung eyes a few months before had softened to a soothing breeze. As the sun welcomed the newly blossoming trees and flowers into its cozy embrace, a celebration of color was beginning to explode - the reward for surviving another brutal Boston winter.

On the sidewalk she breathed in a waft of fresh aromas that triggered a rush of spring fever. A few feet away an elderly vendor hawked single roses left over from Mother's Day.

"Yo, how much?" asked Jazmin.

"Normally three. But for you, sweetie, two dollars."

She parted with her lunch money, selected a velvety red rose, and with a delicate tenderness, held it to her chest.

"Thanks; it's so beautiful."

"I only sell the best, my dear."

The petite teen with cinnamon skin and long, flowing black hair stood at the intersection next to the subway station and looked to the right. About a quarter mile away, her massive high school buzzed with students rushing in from all directions, trying to beat the final bell. Gazing to the left, she eyed a familiar urban park. Surely she could convince Mr. Hunter to let her make up the geometry test so her A+ average could hold firm. She'd play on the mutual crush that had bloomed between young teacher and star student in February, just when the purple spring crocuses were popping up through the snow. Jazmin swooned over the seductive power of his mind; how he, son of Pythagoras, led her into his world of logic, order, and clarity; an oasis in the urban jungle. The fact that he was gay made for safe flirting – head flirting.

She crossed the street toward the park. A low-riding Toyota pulled over and beeped twice: two young men, leering and trying to provoke a reaction.

"Mami, te amo," yelled the driver, the Bachata bursting out the open window.

As a shapely Latina, Jazmin was conditioned to ignore these regular harassments and refused to make eye contact. She continued along one of the two asphalt paths that snaked through the healthy grass almost parallel to each other — one for pedestrians and the other for bicyclists. Jazmin wasn't aware she was on the bike path until a bearded white professional whizzed by, missing her by inches.

"Bike path," he shouted.

"Fuck you," Jazmin screamed back, giving him the finger, which he saw when his helmeted head looked back.

"Stay off the bike path," he ordered, pedaling into the distance.

"Why are white people such assholes?" she mumbled.

Fuming, Jazmin spit, as if ejecting venom and then laughed out loud at the ugly exchange. With her heart still racing from the near collision, she moved a few feet over to the pedestrian path. She felt a pang of guilt for skipping school, but fought it off by rationalizing that she needed a break. For the past week she had been an emotional cyclone, wrecking havoc with friends, family, and teachers. Her history teacher, Mr. Cruz, had almost suspended her after she called him a dick. Luckily, after she profusely apologized, he gave her five days detention instead. Her boyfriend Victor, a convenient target for her uglier projections, got shut down on Saturday night. When he begged for his regular hand job, Jazmin flat out refused, barking "go do your own business." And of course, Jazmin's mother bore the greatest brunt of her chaotic fire.

"Jesus Christ, Mami, I'm not your slave," Jazmin hissed

when her mother commanded her to vacuum the hallway. Without hesitation, Dona Ana Maria slapped her; not once, but twice, leaving a red imprint of her calloused hand on the teen's cheek.

"Don't you ever use the Lord's name like that in my house," Ana Maria threatened, leaning in, daring Jazmin to retaliate.

Struggling to find her voice in a cascade of tears, Jazmin wailed, "I'll call DSS and put you in jail, you abuser. You can't hit me."

"That's what's wrong with this country," her mother retorted. "Teenagers think they're too good to work. You need a good beating, not just a slap."

Her mother complained that she was becoming too "Americanized." But how could Jazmin do otherwise? If her mother didn't want her to be American, they should have stayed in El Salvador.

Jazmin had stormed out of the house, leaving Ana Maria to spend Mother's Day without the presence of her eldest daughter. The growing cultural schism between the two added another heavy layer of stress to the already rocky road that mothers and teen daughters must traverse.

"Even Americanas have to do housework!" her mother had bellowed after her.

Jazmin arrived at her destination: the park's basketball court, deserted and silent at this early hour. She sat on the corner of a two-foot stone wall that formed the perimeter of the court, feeling the vibration of a subway train thundering by in a tunnel twenty feet below. A row of forsythias behind her wove a blanket of bright yellow that glowed in the morning sun, and across the court a bed of red tulips basked in spring's arrival. This was corner where he always sat to rest in between games, sweat steaming off his ripped body. People get comfortable in their spot, and this was his; it was also where the stain of his blood remained etched in the granite slab. Here was the one place on earth where Jazmin felt close to her cousin Bomba. She had tried going to the cemetery, but couldn't feel the intimacy when surrounded by hundreds of graves.

Only four weeks before, in the late afternoon, he had been running the court with his boys and sat down to gulp a Gatorade. A stranger in a navy hoodie calmly glided across the court and approached the sweaty crew of street ball players. They viewed the young man with mild curiosity—until he pulled a nine-millimeter Glock out of his sweatshirt and fired four bullets into Bomba's gut at point-blank range. The shooter waved his gun and shouted threats as the others screamed and scattered, diving into the bushes in panic. Bomba had staggered out to mid-court, where he fell and within minutes bled to death. Ten minutes later the paramedics arrived to find him without a pulse. In the mayhem, it was later reported, the young assassin had sprinted away to a waiting stolen car a few blocks away. The car sped about a half mile, to another stolen car. This one delivered the hit man to the Greyhound bus station, where he collected his $4,500 in cash before heading back to the Bronx.

The park's maintenance crew had arrived at 6:00 AM, exactly a week after the incident, and removed the makeshift memorial: dozens of tired flower bouquets and hundreds of candles, arranged within a huge circle of empty beer, wine, and cognac bottles. The workers applied a fresh coat of paint to the court, covering Bomba's blood and dozens of graffiti messages: "RIP Bomba," "Watch over us, Bomba," "Motherfuckers will pay," "We won't sleep until we find you," "I miss you Bomba," "Love you always, Bomba," "Bomba lives."

Maybe the authorities hadn't seen the bloodstains on the granite slab that served as both a bench for basketball players and a retaining wall for the forsythias. Or maybe they just didn't know how to remove blood from stone. They also hadn't bothered to take down Bomba's sneakers, which decorated the elm tree at the end of the court. The boys had asked Bomba's devastated mother for the shoes and she complied, giving up three pairs. Jazmin had distinct memories of each pair. Bomba had been very particular about his footwear.

The sun's rays started to reach Bomba's spot, and Jazmin ran her fingers over the bloodstain. She knew that with heavy rain showers and a strong sun, the stain would likely fade over the next month.

"Bomba," she said aloud, "where are you?"

As if in reply, she heard the familiar sound of a bouncing basketball on the far end of the court. Looking up, she chuckled.

"Hey, Jamal, what the hell are you doin here?"

The tall, wiry dark-skinned teen dribbled towards her.

"Damn, Jazmin, what the hell are *you* doin here?"

"I'm taking a mental health day. You're not going to school either?"

"Well, it's after seven, and I'm goin to get detention whether I show up now or at eight-thirty, so I figured I'd shoot a few hoops. I guess that makes even more sense now, since I couldn't have copied my Spanish homework from you. So waz up?"

"Just chillin." She smiled.

"You just gonna sit here?"

"Yeah, I like it here. You know, this is where my cousin Bomba got shot."

"Oh yeah, that's right. Bomba was your cousin. Sorry, I forgot. You was close, no?"

"Yeah, we lived together for a few years in my aunt's apartment in the projects. You know Latino families — all packed in together. We were real close."

Jamal gave a sympathetic nod. "I wasn't like super close with him, but we played ball together. That day they shot him? I just left about fifteen minutes before. But man, I came back when I seen those helicopters buzzing all over the park. Ambulance had already taken him, but everyone said he was done."

"Yeah, that day sucked. I wasn't here either, thank god. I don't need those pictures in my mind, but I wish I could have said good-bye."

"Man, Bomba was mad popular. Saint Joseph's was packed at his funeral. Then the mad drinking down here for days. No one went to school. They just sat here and drank; everyone crazy."

Jazmin shrugged. "Crazy, all right. Bomba had it all going. He was eighteen, good-looking; everyone loved him. He had his choice of girls. Boy could rap...he was startin to perform in the clubs. Some people said he could get a basketball scholarship. I miss him, but I'm still mad at him. He started the shit that got him killed. True, Flaco finished it, but Bomba started it."

Jamal sat down beside Jazmin, holding the basketball between his feet. "I heard about it. He whipped Flaco's ass in front of Dunkin' Donuts. Kicked his butt all the way down Centre Street and bloodied him up. Even Flaco's bitch was trying to jump in, whacking Bomba. Bomba should have known that Flaco don't play."

"Yeah, what was he thinkin, kickin Flaco's ass in front of a crowd? That's all anyone talked about for days. Didn't take long for Flaco to get his payback. He was so slick. On the day Bomba got taken out, Flaco was at the hospital in the ER saying he was dizzy – so he had a perfect alibi while he paid his New York boy to do the hit. People say Flaco's scared now, though. No one's seen him; he's laying low. You know someone's gonna fuck him up, and the shit will continue. He's a walking bull's-eye."

Jazmin sighed. "Ayee, Jamal. Why did Bomba even mess with Flaco? Just to get a rep? What the fuck good is a rep when you're dead? Bomba was already the king of his crew, and everything had been cool between Maple and High Street. I guess he got addicted to the rush of power, but that kind of power is like a drug. It's an illusion. It's bullshit. It's what got him k-killed," she said as her voice cracked.

"Fuckin crazy. You miss him, right, Jaz?" said Jamal, gently putting his arm around her shoulder.

Jazmin leaned in and swallowed hard. "Yeah, we was tight. He was a few years older than me and always treated me like his little sister. He called me Mariposa. When we lived together I was in fifth grade, and I did a science project on butterflies. He helped me put it together and he called me Mariposa ever since. I remember we read all about the monarch butterfly and how it migrates to Central America in the winter and then flies all the way back to North America in the spring. Imagine those little butterflies making a trip that long. He used to joke that me and him were like butterflies, since we migrated from El Salvador when we were young."

Jamal smiled. "Pretty word. Mariposa."

"Bomba taught me to play basketball, too," Jazmin added, sitting up. "He would take me down here to chill. Sometimes we'd be the first to get here and we'd shoot around, play one-on-one for fun." She gazed at the blood-red tulips, then took a deep whiff of her rose.

"I miss him a lot, and I miss the others too. I've lost so many homies, Jamal. You know how it goes: first the shock, then in line at the wake, the candles, the flowers, the funeral, the mothers and aunts screaming, collapsing in the church. The speeches by the community leaders and priests, the television cameras. Then all the drama queens; suddenly the dude is everybody's best friend, and bitches who barely knew him are acting out like he was the fucking love of their miserable lives. Then all the drinking and talk of revenge. The buttons, the T-shirts. And a week or a month later, the retaliation, and someone else is dead. I'm so tired of it. What did I go to, about eight funerals this year? I'm not goin anymore. I'm tired."

"I hear you."

"I miss them all, but Bomba, he was family. I never lost family before. When you grow up with someone, when you live with them, you know them so well. Bomba was popular because of his laugh, his jokes, his moves on the court, his charm with the ladies. But I truly knew him. We were so close. So I come here to feel Bomba; it helps, it makes me strong."

Jamal turned to her, shaking his head. "These things take time, Jazmin."

"I know. I have so many memories. I never had a brother. I never had a father, either. Maybe that's why he was so special. When he got his license he took me out in my aunt's car and taught me how to drive. I was thirteen and driving all over Boston. I could barely see over the steering wheel. I remember one time on Columbus Ave. I pulled up next to a Boston cop. He looked right into my eyes. Asshole was either stupid or didn't give a fuck, cause he just drove off. Bomba took me on his business rounds. You know, he was dealing a lot of weed, but he never let me try it."

"Speaking of weed, it's time for breakfast." Jamal chuckled as he pulled a half joint out of his pocket, and lit up. "You sure you don't want some?" he asked with a wink.

"I'm good; but I do like the smell." Rather than inhale the sweet smoke, Jazmin breathed deeply of her rose.

"You know, Jamal, when Bomba's boy Oscar got shot a few months ago, I started to get real scared," she said. "It seemed there was a shooting every week for a while. I sat Bomba down and I made him promise me he wouldn't do anything stupid. He said, 'Don't worry, Mariposa, I'll be around.' But he's not around, at least not in body."

"You religious, Jaz? I mean, like, you think Bomba's spirit is still around?"

"I *know* he's still around. I can't explain it. You know, I'm Catholic, and we believe in heaven, purgatory, and hell. I want to think that Bomba is in purgatory, where people have to pay for their sins before they go to heaven. God knows that Bomba committed sins. He did some bad shit, but he had a good side too, a sweet side, a generous side. I think I knew his sweet side better than anyone. He did a lot for me and he did a lot for his family. But you know something, Jamal? Even though I'm Catholic, I kind of believe in reincarnation. I asked Father Flaherty about it; he's a good guy, not one of the perverts. Anyway, he told me flat out no. But I don't trust everything those priests say."

Jamal shook his head. "I don't trust any of them. The minister at my grandmother's church is a hustler. She's always givin him money she doesn't have."

"Yeah, I don't go to church much, but I've read some books about Hinduism — you know, the ancient religion of India. The Hindus believe that humans have a soul that continues living after death, and that we come down to Earth in one life after another to learn lessons. In between lives, we rest and reflect on what we learned in the previous life. This makes sense to me; maybe I'm a Catholic Hindu."

Jamal grinned and blew out a soft stream of smoke.

"Anyway, when I come here, I can feel Bomba," Jazmin said. "I get the same feeling I always had when he was with me—his warmth, his protection. So I do believe his spirit still exists. And he sure needs to learn some lessons from his last life. He really fucked it up. But I know he didn't want to die, and I also know he's feeling a lot of pain now cause he hurt all of us. Are you religious, Jamal?"

"No, not really." Jamal took his last hit from the joint that had all but disappeared between his fingers. "My mom stopped taking me to church when I was eight. I guess at that point she thought I was old enough to stay home and watch cartoons with my brothers and sisters. I want to believe there's a god, but I just don't know. When one of my boys gets killed, I feel real bad. Everyone talks about heaven. I hear the adults praying and stuff, but I myself just feel sad for a while. Then it kinds of fades and things are back to normal again. But you keep wondering what happened to the dude. If he can really look down on us."

"Jamal, I really like you. You seem like you have a good head, even if you fuck it all up with weed. Please don't be the next one to get shot."

"I'll be okay, Jazmin. I know how to keep it cool." Jamal stood and gave the basketball a few bounces. "I should head down to school. You sure you don't want to go?"

"No, I'll go in tomorrow."

"Okay, Jazzie. I hope you don't get too sad here. You're too pretty a girl to be sad." He leaned in to get a kiss on the cheek, a ritual that had worked its way into the urban teen culture, imported by the Latino kids.

"Later, Jamal."

"Later, Jazz," he said as he floated onto the bicycle path, dribbling his ball.

Now the morning sun fully embraced Bomba's corner. Jazmin

stretched out her body on the stone wall, using her backpack as a pillow. She held her rose inches from her eyes. She felt drawn into the mystical cavern of deep red between the petals, pulled by its simple and divine beauty. Accepting the invitation to enter into its mystery, she merged her consciousness with nature's love symbol and drifted off . . . .

She sat on a stunningly beautiful beach, playing in the sand at the water's edge. Without warning, black clouds rolled in and a huge tidal wave surged, racing toward the shoreline. Terrified, she started to run, but the wave broke over her. She was tumbling, thrashing in the foam, choking and coughing up the salty water. Just when darkness and despair set in, two strong arms pulled her up and sat her back on the shore. The wave had passed and the beach shone with a clear sunny brilliance, radiating a deep tranquility. She gazed out into the sparkling ocean, and there was Bomba waving, diving in and out of the water like a dolphin.

Maybe it was the intensity of the dream, or maybe the subway train rumbling underneath, but Jazmin woke with a pounding heart.

"Bomba," she whispered, as a single tear of gratitude slid down her cheek, landing on his bloodstain. Grasping the long-stemmed rose, she lightly pricked her thumb on a thorn and added a droplet of her own blood to the mix.

She left the rose on the wall and walked towards school.

Substitute

Hey, easy money, I thought. The Boston Public Schools paid substitute teachers seventy-five bucks a day. The deal went like this: you applied, got approved, and your name appeared on an availability list. Then you waited for a principal to call.

Twenty-three years old with a college degree, I qualified. I earned a meager hundred bucks a week writing freelance news articles and needed more cash to keep up with my expenses: rent, food, utilities, student loans, beer and weed.

Three days after filing my application in the Human Resources office, I got a call at 6:30 on a Monday morning. More than slightly hung-over, I showered quickly and trotted down to the subway. My career as a substitute teacher had officially kicked-off. I arrived at the Lincoln Elementary School and reported to the main office. There a frazzled administrator – a bald dude with big wads of hair on each side of his skull -- slapped some folders in my hands and barked incoherent instructions. Once I found my assigned room, I got a disdainful glare from the teacher's aide who was temporarily covering and waiting for me. The absent teacher had left some kind of busywork—boring, tedious worksheets that I handed out. The racially mixed group of kids still had at least some fear of a male with a loud authoritarian voice, so I kept order -- my primary responsibility.

For about two weeks I catapulted around the city, filling in at elementary and middle schools, providing mostly glorified babysitting. I learned quickly that a substitute teacher embodied the lowest of the low in the school's food chain; lower than the lazy fat gym teachers, way below the psychotic security guards and several levels beneath the cranky lunch mothers, the heavily medicated janitors and the bellowing, hateful bus drivers. Teachers and administrators either ignored me or directed disgusted looks my way as I went about my humble duties. The fact that I didn't look like your typical school teacher might have had something to do with the icy reception. I wore construction boots, jeans, and whatever T-shirt was available under my black leather jacket. My hair resembled a rat's nest, at times covered by a Scally cap, and I had a formidable beard. Some of my friends referred to me as Jesus Christ, while others fondly addressed me as Charlie — Manson, that is.

With two categories of teachers in the Boston Public Schools, I fit into neither. About seventy percent were Caucasian, over fifty years old, and burnt out. Several of the white-haired Irish males had serious drinking problems, evidenced by their rosy cheeks, grotesque, chewed-up noses, and their constant popping of mints, which never quite covered up the whiskey. The remaining thirty percent consisted of younger Latinos and blacks – none of whom seemed to be on the lookout for white friends.

In an act of self-preservation, I avoided interaction with adults inside the school buildings. I didn't want, nor need, their acceptance, and I refused to be a target for their pent-up stress and anger, which they freely projected my way. Whenever I had an open period I found a quiet corner where I could read or edit a newspaper article.

This outcast status in the schools complemented my developing identity as an offbeat intellectual. During my early and adolescent years I had belonged to the brotherhood of athletes and thugs over in Charlestown, a densely populated working-class Irish-Catholic enclave tucked away in a northern corner of Boston. After high school many of the old gang had joined the ranks of the Irish mafia, or "wise guys." Several others had entered law enforcement, and now they were thugs in uniforms. By day, these two groups supposedly battled each other; but by night they actually drank together in various seedy pubs.

What set me apart from my blood brothers was that I read.

Call me a bibliophile; I just loved books. I never wanted to be different, but it was this intellectual passion that ultimately freed me from the confining, stifling collective consciousness of our homogenous urban community. I like to lose myself in a book, talk about books, and hang out with people who read them. Unfortunately, most of my childhood crowd thought James Joyce was either the name of a downtown pub or a new Irish whiskey.

The identity change from Townie to intellectual picked up steam after I went cross town to the Jesuit-run Boston College and entered the more adventurous world of ideas. I took courses in psychology, sociology, literature, political science, and history, all of which I found fascinating. My left-leaning dorky professors won me over with their sharp, critical analysis of American culture and politics. Through them I developed a social consciousness impossible to explain to my fellow Townies. In Charlestown we had simple politics: Support labor unions, God bless America, tax the rich, and bomb the hell out of any country that wants to fuck with us. Oh yeah, and one more: round up the illegals, send them back, and seal the border.

The wide range of females available at the university provided another great motivator for identity exploration. I found that as an "intellectual" I had access to a greater variety of young co-eds than did the typical working-class stiff whose concept of reading the paper consisted of checking the Red Sox box scores. I learned about the scores of beautiful, promiscuous women who attached themselves to these green, leftist political movements; it seemed my consciousness expanded with each new sexual adventure.

So my need for intellectual *and* sexual stimulation — mind and body — lured me out of the cozy comfort of Charlestown's tight-knit community. After graduating from B.C., I went through the ridiculous roommate interview process and migrated to the culturally diverse, funky eclectic neighborhood of Jamaica Plain from where I launched my career as a substitute. I did miss the beer chugging, party dancing, corner hanging, hockey stick swinging, car stealing, Bunker Hill Day celebrating, bar brawling, dope peddling, pill popping, bet making, pool playing, leg breaking, project-girl screwing, pistol whipping, street-fighting excitement of an adrenaline-laced lifestyle. No doubt about it, for young thugs, Charlestown epitomized the center of the universe. Never a dull moment, drama ruled; unresolved primitive tensions, threats, and paybacks kept our blood pumping and confirmed our existence. I often went back to the bars for short visits and fit right back in: Once a Townie, always a Townie.

I found a shabby apartment with two graduate students. Rob, from Venezuela, studied at Berklee College of Music. Susan, a twenty-six-year-old black woman from Detroit, was pursuing a law degree at Northeastern.

I rarely saw Rob, but Susan and I hung out often at home, where we developed an unlikely camaraderie. A voracious reader, she possessed one of the sharpest minds I have ever encountered. She already had a Ph.D. in "Street" after growing up in one of Detroit's most notorious housing projects, where she somehow survived tragedy upon tragedy that her fractured family had suffered. One of the reasons she had chosen to study in Boston was that she wanted to reconnect with a younger half-sister, Tanya, who lived in nearby Dorchester.

Susan exemplified a complementary mix of African and Native American features. Deceptively beautiful with light brown skin, she wore dozens of long braids and loose-fitting jeans and sweatshirts. It wasn't until one day when she came back to the house from a dance class, still in tight clothes, that I noticed her knockout body. Her thin, strong frame was adorned with moderate breasts and an artfully sculptured ass. A sprinter in high school, she still had those Flo-Jo legs. Describing herself as a bisexual, she slept alone most nights, claiming she had no time for relationships. Occasionally Lucia, a Puerto Rican woman in her early thirties, came up from New York to spend a weekend. They had lived together as a couple when Susan was an undergraduate, but now were "close friends who slept together once in a while."

When I first met Susan, she gave me one of those "you're a punk white boy who isn't worth my time" looks. But eventually we became close—well, about as close as a black radical feminist and a working class white boy can get. I do have to credit Susan for giving me a chance. Yes, many members of my old crew in Charlestown were hard-core racists, victims of a social disease they inherited from their parents during the 1970s busing crisis, when Boston was viewed as the world's epicenter of racial hate. Back then black kids beefed with white kids on a daily basis. White mothers from Charlestown and South Boston welcomed young black students into their neighborhood schools by pelting them with stones. If I had a dime for every time I heard the "N" word come out of a white mouth, I'd be set for life. My devout Catholic parents had stayed out of the political fray around busing and never taught me to hate. From my days playing on a citywide basketball team, I felt relatively comfortable around black folks, but it took some time for Susan to get over my whiteness.

We gradually broke through the thick racial divide and bonded because of some common interests. We both liked to wind down at night with a few drinks, we craved discussions on literature and film, and we loved the NBA. Through my literature courses I had read all of Toni Morrison's novels, which gave us endless opportunities to discuss race - Susan's obsession. Since I had also seen all of Spike Lee's films and read just about everything written by Alice Walker, Langston Hughes, Richard Wright, and her favorite - James Baldwin - we had a foundation of common reference points. Because of my capacity to discuss literary themes, stay relaxed around her, and be real, I earned at least some of her trust. This allowed me privileged access to Susan's world—access she had never before made available to a white person.

Striving to be at the top of her class, Susan put in sixteen-hour days. With my substitute teaching, graduate courses, and keeping up with my weekly deadlines, I also had a packed, caffeine-paced schedule. So each night at about ten o'clock we found ourselves at the kitchen table, ready to share either a six-pack or a bottle of wine.

If there was a basketball game on, we'd eventually move to the living room couch. On our most fun nights, Susan's Detroit Pistons played my Boston Celtics.

On the evenings when I had a female visitor – usually about twice a week – Susan would stay holed up in her room. Not once did she make eye contact with my "activist" friends, never mind speak to them or acknowledge their presence.

Susan admitted to having no white friends, no interest in anyone white, and even confessed to me that as a young girl she refused to drink white milk and told a white Santa Claus to fuck himself. She seemed to have a love-hate relationship with black men. She had been married — only for a year and a half — to a brother, and even though she didn't talk much about it, I could sense the lingering, unresolved bitterness. However, Susan passionately defended black men any time the slightest hint of racial bias surfaced on TV. She often railed against the criminal justice system that had put her father and thousands like him behind bars.

Susan sensed that I found her attractive, but I knew to keep my distance. She made it so clear that African-Americans and whites could never attain a genuine intimate relationship; just too much historical baggage, she explained. I began to understand that when Susan looked at me, she saw a descendent of a slave master who had raped female slaves. I wanted to think that Susan and I could start a friendship with a clean slate, removed and independent from the past. But from her perspective, I had been stained with the original sin of being born white. Somehow, though, through all the racial history and complexes, we managed to enjoy each other's company for a couple of hours most nights. In particular, Susan seemed to love hearing about the everyday adventures of a Boston substitute teacher as we sipped on our drinks.

After about a month of working in elementary and middle schools, they sent me to a high school located just a few blocks from my apartment. Roosevelt High – a poster child for our apartheid-like education system - had gained a notorious reputation as a dangerous and failing urban school. Ninety percent of the students were low-income African-Americans and Latinos, and the dropout rate stood at over forty percent. At about 7:00 AM every morning, a thousand students passed through metal detectors, and it seemed more security guards and police strolled the corridors than teachers.

My first assignment had me at a hallway table in the role of a semi-security guard, signing male students in and out of a bathroom. The teens didn't know what to make of me. They knew I wasn't a cop, but my boyish looks, wild hair, and street clothes threw them off. While mildly confused, they possessed not the slightest bit of curiosity. I was a benign, harmless alien, just another strange white person that they bumped into within institutional walls.

On my second day they assigned me to a study hall. Through the six periods, the room stayed pretty much empty. A few Asian kids huddled in small groups doing homework. The black and Latino students entered the room, took one look at me, pointed, laughed, and skipped back out into the corridor to God knows where. I took attendance, but no one ever collected it. At midday during my free period, I ventured out into the hallway to see how I could get into one of the locked-up teacher's bathrooms. After five teachers refused to loan me their key, I approached a student bathroom, where few adults dared to go. I entered during class time, so it was empty except for one student who stood in front of a urinal a few feet away. A tall, good-looking black kid, he wore a thick down coat. A do-rag covered his head and hung down the back of his neck. A cloud of smoke surrounded his upper body. I immediately recognized the delicious pungent aroma. With glazed light brown eyes he stared at me and took a long thoughtful hit. After he exhaled, in a low raspy voice he said, "Yo, you want some?" as more smoke curled towards me.

"No thanks," I replied.

He gazed at me with a perplexed countenance. "Yo, man, you're not a teacher, are you?"

"Yes," I said. "I am."

He bolted past me out the door, and I dutifully followed him, assuming I had the responsibility to bust this kid. I followed from a safe distance to the end of the empty corridor on the first floor. Looking back at me, he could see I wasn't bluffing. Without hesitation he pushed on an emergency exit door and disappeared into the white of the snow-covered winter morning. I looked behind me and saw not a soul; good. Now no one could blame me for his infraction.

As I hurried down the corridor back to my classroom, I suddenly halted at the sight of a middle-aged white female teacher on her knees, sobbing in front of a row of lockers. As she ranted on about how the students tortured her, one of her colleagues appeared out of a nearby classroom to console her. Security guards, mumbling into walkie-talkies, appeared dumbfounded. The nightmarish scene sent a chill through my chest. I found out later that Ms. O'Conner had suffered a nervous breakdown and went out on a long sick leave.

A few days after Ms. O'Conner's meltdown, a disheveled, anxiety-ridden, wild-eyed assistant principal wearing a tired, wrinkled, stained brown suit sent me to the cafeteria for lunch duty. Over a dozen teachers and security guards were posted around the perimeter, every twenty or thirty yards, theoretically to maintain order as the kids gobbled up their stale ham sandwiches and wrinkled green beans. I stood at my assigned space, trying to decide if the school more resembled a prison or an asylum. I fought the urge to break open the exit doors and scream, "Run, run."

Without warning a loud exchange erupted at a table just to the right of me. One kid threw a half-full milk carton into another student's face. The milk-covered student hurled himself over the table onto the thrower, causing him to fall back in his chair. Within seconds, all four hundred students were clambering toward ground zero, cheering, jeering, and screaming for action.

Never in my life had I seen such frenzy. The bulled-over kid on the floor got up slowly, a bit dazed. But in a flash, he grabbed his folding metal chair, muscled it over his head, and began charging toward his enemy. From my position about ten feet away, I realized that no one planned to intervene. I sprinted from my post and tackled the chair holder from behind before he inflicted damage. The two of us rolled over each other on the floor, the chair slamming down a few feet from our heads. Once we were down, several armed security guards swooped in and took the two perpetrators into custody.

"What are you, fucking crazy?" said one of the punk security guards, getting in my face like the whole incident was my fault.

"I'm crazy, motherfucker? Wasn't I doing your fucking job?" I fired back, as adrenaline pulsed through my veins. I moved toward him glaring, daring him to say more, and he backed off as teachers herded the students back to class.

A young, shapely Puerto Rican teacher approached me. "Thank God you acted. That could have gotten real ugly," she said with a strong, sexy accent. Then she sashayed away, no doubt aware I was watching with admiration. "Nice job," she added as she smiled over her shoulder.

"Ah, thanks, talk to you later," I yelled down the corridor, making a mental note to find out where her classroom was. Up to that moment I had never considered that getting ass could be a benefit of this job.

My simple, apparently heroic act earned me a short-lived modicum of notoriety in the school. As I walked through the crowded corridors in the following days, several of the students recognized me, saying, "Hey, cuz, waz up?"

The early morning calls from the Roosevelt principal continued, and I took on the status of a "permanent sub." Due to the high rate of teacher absenteeism – probably related to alcoholism - they actually needed me. Although increasingly comfortable, my survival instincts remained on high alert. I waited with anticipation for the next calamity, which came faster than I imagined.

About two weeks after the cafeteria incident I covered a history class. During the period just before lunch, a crowd of students streamed into the classroom. To my amazement, nearly every seat in the room filled. I called the attendance roll, but no one raised a hand. I did notice the tall marijuana smoker with his do-rag sitting in the back of the room, but we conveniently ignored each other. Double-checking the attendance list, I made sure it was the right time period. After going through the entire list again, I asked a male in the front row his name.

"Joe Johnson, sir."

I wrote it down and nodded to the student behind him. "And your name?"

"Joseph Johnson, sir."

I tried one more male: "J. Johnson, sir."

"Hmmm," I muttered. I looked to my right and addressed a light-skinned black girl. "What's your name?"

"Josephine Johnson, sir." She smiled.

"Wow!" I chuckled. "One big happy family. Are you all just back from the Johnson Family Reunion?"

Except for a few repressed giggles, the students remained stoic, sitting upright with their hands folded on the desks, their eyes straight ahead. Moving on, I passed out worksheets left by their teacher. At any moment I expected the entire Johnson clan to get up and walk out of the room, but surprisingly, everyone stayed. Befuddled, I pulled the latest issue of *Newsweek* out of my backpack and began reading.

I don't know the exact order in which the following happened, because the events occurred within seconds: the windowless classroom grew pitch black and a rapid breeze ruffled my hair, followed by a violent bang behind me. Sitting in the blinding darkness, I heard another thunderous boom. Then came the rapid fire. With the instincts of a cat, I fell to my knees and crept under the large metal teacher's desk. For what seemed an eternity, hundreds of textbooks slammed against the chalkboard behind me. An occasional one pounded my protective barrier. Curled up, with my arms covering my head, I felt the violent vibrations rattling my spine.

After a full minute, the deafening noise abruptly ended. Apparently, the Johnsons had run out of ammo. I remained in a fetal position under the desk, waiting for something to happen, as an eerie silence reigned. Remembering that I was responsible and in charge of the room, I eased out from my cover with great caution and crawled ever so quietly toward the red exit sign above the door. Feeling the way up along the wall, my hand found the light switch. I scanned the scene, and all twenty students sat at their desks, staring ahead with their hands folded. My desk and the surrounding floor were littered with hundreds of old history textbooks that just minutes before had been neatly stacked in bookcases. The chalkboard behind me had cracked in several places.

In shock, I remained kneeling near the light switch until the principal, Mr. Martin, burst in. A huge black man, Martin stood at six foot four inches and weighed over three hundred pounds. A massive thick roll of accumulated fat on the lower back of his bald head curled like a wave when he strutted through the corridors. Panting incessantly, he wore thick glasses and a tailored suit with a bowtie.

"What in the name of God happened here?" he roared.

"I wish I knew," I responded meekly from the floor.

He picked up some books and stacked them on my desk.

"What is your name?" he shouted. Sweat broke out across his brow. I had never seen a black man's face so red.

"Mathew Mulligan, substitute," I answered.

"Mr. Mulligan, please come out into the hallway."

I followed him out to the corridor, where he proceeded to lambaste me. He threatened to fire me, and swore that if anything like this happened again, he would personally make sure that I never set foot again in a Boston Public School. Worst of all, the students gleefully heard the whole tirade. I silently accepted his venom and then watched him waddle down the corridor, raving, spitting, and huffing.

As soon as Martin was out of sight, all except three of the extended Johnson family slid out the door and disappeared, no doubt off to celebrate one of the greatest substitute-abuse pranks of all time. Not only had they come dangerously close to destroying me physically and fracturing my nerves, but they had almost gotten me fired.

I deduced that the lingering students were not part of the

conspiracy. As I restacked the books, a petite Latina girl with a cross hanging from her neck stooped down to help.

"Thank you," I said.

"Mister," she said in a whisper, as she knelt down next to me. "Do you promise not to say anything?"

"Sure," I responded.

"It was Jamal who did that. He had it all planned. That's why everyone came to class. Mr. Humphrey, our history teacher, told us yesterday that he was going to be out and that we'd have a sub. That's when Jamal started to talk to everyone and tell them what to do. Mister, I hate Jamal, but he'll kill me if he knows that I told you."

"Thank you for this information," I said softly. "Which student is Jamal? What does he look like?"

"He sat right there," she said, pointing to the last seat and the closest one to the rear light switch and the bookcases.

"The tall black kid with the do-rag and down coat?"

"Yes, mister, that's Jamal, Jamal Hunter."

So now I knew the name of my dope-smoking friend. "Okay," I said, "don't worry; this is our secret. I don't even know your name, and I don't want to. Jamal will pay for this, but he'll never know it was you."

She looked around nervously. "Okay, mister. I'm sorry. You didn't deserve this."

"Thanks again. Now you'd better get going to your next class."

Rage replaced the shock and overtook me. I forced myself to take deep breaths. I struggled to control my impulse to race through the corridors, seek him out, kick him to the ground, drag him by his do-rag to the office, throw him on top of the principal, and then pummel the both of them. Yes, Jamal was tall, athletic, and obviously nuts, but I knew that fueled with vengeance and adrenaline, I could easily overpower his thin frame. I paced inside the empty classroom, trying to control and organize my dark thoughts. All of my street instincts roared. I looked for a stick, a pipe, anything that would serve as a weapon to take out Jamal. But I checked my anger, knowing it would only lead to trouble. Big trouble . . . court trouble . . . jail trouble. By God's grace, as I continued to circle the room, reason eased into to my chemically charged brain. I had to be patient and wait. Delicate situations require thoughtful strategy.

Details of my near-death experience tore through the social fabric of the institution, to the delight of all. I found it impossible to walk down the corridor later that day without evoking catcalls, snickers, giggles, and outright howling. I actually caught a teacher in the hallway pointing at me while giggling with a group of students. In the cafeteria I noticed black and Latino lunch mothers and security guards leaning towards each other and bursting into laughter. It seemed the whole school was enjoying my nightmare. Later that night I tried to assess the situation, but my thoughts raced, logic driven out. I drank a bottle of wine, and then another. I recounted the horror to Susan, but found no empathy.

"Of course these kids will act out," she said. "It is a legitimate human response to being treated like caged animals."

I didn't have the energy to argue with her.

Feeling helpless and humiliated, I called in sick the remainder of the week. During those initial nights I lay in a torturous, half-sleepless state with Jamal hovering above me, mocking me with the ugliest of laughs. His image took on gigantic proportions, and I felt like Dorothy, cowering before the Wizard of Oz. I pondered the nature of revenge, wondering if this human instinct is inherently evil or liberating. Even though I had not practiced the Catholic faith for years, I figured maybe the Bible could help me understand the overpowering drive for vengeance. But I found only contradictory passages. The first was Psalm 127:8-9, which said: "O daughter of Babylon, doomed to destruction, happy is he who repays you for what you have done to us; he who seizes your young infants and thrashes them against the rocks." And then there was Leviticus 19:18: "Thou shalt not avenge nor bear any grudge against the children of thy people, but thou shalt love thy neighbor as thy self."

Me love Jamal? I preferred to think of thrashing him against rocks. Maybe, I reasoned, revenge allowed nature to keep order in the universe. It does satisfy, but where does it lead? Could I ever forgive Jamal without first evening the score?

I did believe in the law of karma and divine retribution—or, put more simply, "What goes around, comes around"—but I lacked the patience to wait for God's intervention. I thought of the Furies from the Greek and Roman myths. Female spirits of justice and vengeance, under Zeus's command they would appear as storm clouds and swarms of insects, torturing and tormenting until the wrongdoer showed remorse; not until then would they would let up. I could take on the role of the furies, yes. But how would I get Jamal to express remorse?

After a few days of wine and nursing my very existence, I achieved clarity: Jamal would pay. I would have my revenge. Emboldened now to the point of obsession, new energy poured into my psyche. I had a dream; I had a dream that one day Jamal would get on his knees and beg for forgiveness; I had a dream that one day justice would be served – by any means necessary. I relished the thought of being the judge, jury, and executioner.

But my new identity and the past roiled in deep conflict. I may have evolved into a politically correct pseudo-intellectual, but I had a Townie soul, and no one fucked with a Townie. I could read books, go to college, and experience diversity, but at my core the Townie dominated. If Jamal's attack had happened on the street, a simple set of rules would apply. But inside the school I forced myself to think through my options. At one level I understood that there were a plethora of reasons why Satan himself had moved in and occupied the insidious soul of this handsome young kid. But when these sympathetic thoughts swirled, my inner Townie squashed any humanistic impulses.

I returned to work, and the buzz of my near-catastrophe subsided. Whenever Jamal saw me he'd give me a cocky, loud greeting: "Hey, cuz!" I quietly stared into his eyes, knowing he hadn't a clue that the Latina had given him up. I maintained control and waited. But how, I pondered, and when, would I make my move?

A solution appeared suddenly and spontaneously. I had learned that the school gym stood empty for about an hour after the last bell, so every afternoon I took advantage of the space to practice martial arts. I had studied a form of Shaolin kung fu for several years and craved going through a daily workout.

While going through an intense thirty-minute routine of jumps, punches, kicks, and blocks, I became aware that someone sat in the bleachers watching me. I continued the exercise, however, with all of my energy focused inward. By the time I finished, I was panting, with sweat pouring from my body. I looked across the gym, and there sat Jamal with a big grin.

"Yo teach," he said as he swaggered my way. "That was pretty cool. I didn't know you was into the arts."

"What are you doing here, Jamal?" I asked coldly. He seemed surprised that I knew his name.

"Just waiting for basketball practice." He jerked his chin toward my old Townie Scally cap, which sat on the gym floor beside my backpack. An old Charlestown girlfriend - Molly O'Brien, a red-head - had sown a green shamrock onto it several years before.

"Yo teach, you from South Boston or something?"

"No, Charlestown," I responded, "but it's a lot like Southie."

"Charlestown, huh. There's a lot of gang killing over there. You all got that code of silence."

"Gee, Jamal, I'm surprised that you know about my turf. What, do you read the *Boston Herald*?"

"No, I saw a special about it on TV the other night."

Another basketball player called to Jamal from the locker room.

"Okay, teach, later," he said, strutting away.

"Jamal, come here," I ordered with authority. I wore the subtlest of smiles as he obeyed and sauntered back. "I've been meaning to talk to you, Jamal. You know that book-throwing incident a few weeks ago? Those books were heavy, and if one had hit me it could have really fucked me up."

He stared at me, his bloodshot eyes growing wider, his mouth hanging open. His left cheek twitched. Up to that moment, he'd clearly thought he'd pulled off the perfect crime. I moved closer so our faces were inches apart.

"Those books just missed my head, my eyes," I continued. "I could have spent months in the hospital, you son of a bitch. I imagine you think highly of yourself for orchestrating that scheme."

He stood mute and backed up a few feet. I followed, maintaining the tight distance; this was the most intimate of conversations.

"You gotta understand something, Jamal. If any of my crew — and believe me, I know a lot of wise guys — hear about what you did, do you have any idea what they will do to you? I'm just going to say one thing Jamal: You'd better watch your back. This is not over."

He gazed at me with puppy eyes; his fragile cockiness frittered away. It felt good, real good. I had handily won the psychological battle. I'd scared the shit out of him. Now instead of him being in my head, I owned his. What a turnaround; what a victory! Through this chance encounter, I had shattered the illusion of his teenage brazenness, just as he had shattered my nerves. Now he stood at my mercy — just where I wanted him.

That night I proudly entered the kitchen, anxious to tell Susan about my triumph. I bought a six-pack of sixteen-ounce Guinness and popped one open. Susan sat down and immediately I related my conversation with Jamal. I expected some mild criticism but I felt confident I would gain her understanding.

"So what you are telling me is that you threatened to hurt him or possibly kill him," she said with a bitter tone.

"Yeah, I guess you could say that."

"You, a so-called professional educator?"

I pushed a Guinness across the table, but she refused. She pulled her hair back as her deepening agitation permeated the kitchen.

"I can't believe you threatened a student. You should go to jail, Matt. This is not only unethical and immoral, but it is illegal. I should call the fucking authorities and report you." Her cheeks burned.

"Hello, Susan, self-defense," I countered. "Are you forgetting that this punk almost killed me? Not with words, but with hard textbooks that could have knocked me unconscious or cracked my skull? Was that immoral or unethical? Talk about double standards. And how about the lack of support from the principal? If I don't defend myself in that war zone, who will? You're giving me a bunch of politically correct bullshit. If white students had pummeled you with books, you'd be raising holy hell and you know it."

"Fuck, Matt, you don't get it, do you? Yeah, Jamal is a punk, but does that give you the right to be a punk too? You responded like a thug."

"Damn it, Susan, I have some pride. If I don't show that I can meet these punks at their level, they'll walk all over me."

"Bullshit. This is about race and your petty need for revenge against a troubled kid."

"How is this about race? If a white student did this to me, I'd respond the same way. I didn't go after Jamal because he's black, I went after him because he tried to fucking hurt me."

"This *is* about race. Jamal went after you, I'm sure, because you are white."

"So he's a racist."

"No, he's a victim of a racist society. And he is channeling his very justified anger in an inappropriate manner. To be honest, I find his actions to be more appropriate than the typical black-on-black violence. At least Jamal, at some level, knows who is oppressing him."

"So I've been oppressing him. Huh. You sure sound just like an out-of-touch academic whack-job."

"No, Matt, I'm very much in touch with all the racist hate of your people. If you are going to work with black and Latino kids, you'd better start understanding their anger. They are carrying around more anger than you could ever imagine. And their anger is very logical and justified. They have grown up in a society where the mainstream culture projects hate and fear onto them twenty-four-seven. What you are doing is very stupid. You may have scared Jamal, and it made you feel good, but what is the outcome? Does it help him with his anger? No. Does it make you safer? No. What happens in two or three years from now if he is running with a gang and carrying a Magnum around town? Do you think he will forget you? No, you will be at the top of his list—the white punk who humiliated him. Trust me, he'll come looking for you. Your words today will perpetuate a cycle of violence that could come back to haunt you."

"Trust me, I'm not afraid of that punk and I never will be," I replied in my most macho of tones.

Susan stormed out and went to her room, slamming the door. But her words stung and struck deep. Desiring her empathy, all I got was her wrath. After downing five more Guinnesses at the kitchen table, I came to the ultimate realization that she was right—at least the part about my behaving unprofessionally. *Shit, I'm a teacher,* I reminded myself, *and I threatened a student.* I experienced a wave of paranoia . . . and then a subtle guilt entered my being. As the beers took their effect, a desire to understand Jamal mysteriously replaced my anger.

I awoke not with a hangover, but pumped with a welcome new energy. In the following days I surreptitiously gathered intelligence on Jamal. A few of the kids in the school had been warming up to me, and they served as reliable sources. In addition, I sought out a burnt-out guidance counselor and a staff social worker. Through all these channels I learned that Jamal was sixteen years old and a freshman. He had spent six months in a juvenile facility for an accumulation of crimes: stealing a bike, driving an unregistered motorcycle, throwing rocks at police cars. His mother was in jail for repeated shoplifting; apparently a strategy to finance her heroin habit. After his father had disappeared years before, Jamal had lived with an uncle who had physically abused him, until DSS got involved. Eventually he ended up living with his wheelchair-bound grandmother.

Yeah, I began to understand Jamal's anger issues. He had gained infamy and popularity in his neighborhood and school as a goofball and a small-time troublemaker. A talented basketball player, he often got benched or suspended for attitude and anger issues. Given his atrocious grades, short of a quick dramatic turnaround, he'd need to repeat freshman year — at age seventeen.

After our curt conversation in the gym, whenever Jamal spotted me in the hallway he darted in the opposite direction. He had taken my threat seriously, and I pondered how I could reopen the avenues of communication. After a couple of cooling-off weeks, I waited in the gym. Sure enough, he came through on his way to basketball.

"Jamal, can I talk to you for a minute?" He stopped and regarded me with both fear and perplexity. "Listen," I continued. "I was pissed off the last time I talked to you, but I want you to know that I'm over it. I'm ready to forget about what happened — to let it go. Sound good to you?"

"Ya, that's cool."

"Jamal, you know, a couple of weeks ago, we were enemies. But sometimes, enemies have a strange way of becoming friends. I'm willing to give it a try. Do you want to pass this year?"

"Yeah, that'd be good. If not, I can't play ball."

"Then let me make you an offer. Every day I come to the gym to work out, but if you get here right after the last bell, I can spend some time helping with homework. I'll leave it up to you, but I'll be here. Just show up with your books and homework if you want help."

"Okay, thanks," he said, shifting his weight before heading off to the locker room.

For the next three days I waited, reading in the bleachers before my workout routine. On the fourth day Jamal strutted in, his backpack filled. We started with a history essay, and from then on he came regularly. I found that while he picked up math and science fairly easily, he struggled with English and social sciences. Jamal confessed to me that he had never read a whole book in his life. Working the school's fractured support system, I made arrangements for Jamal to see a therapist at school every week. Over the course of a semester we got a few of his F's and D's up to C's, and hope stayed alive that he'd pass into sophomore year. After tutoring, our brief conversations focused exclusively on sports—a safe domain for our male bonding. Sometimes, if we found a basketball lying around the gym, we'd post up a quick game of knockout or HORSE.

At the end of the semester, he had an assignment: a five-hundred-word review on a book of his choice. Somehow he ended up skimming through *The Autobiography of Malcolm X*. The paper required a minimal amount of research, and Roosevelt's library closed by the time basketball practice ended. So late one afternoon, I walked Jamal up to the local public library a block away from my apartment. After accomplishing our mission, I invited Jamal to have a snack at my house. When we walked in, Susan's jaw dropped. Ever since our argument a month before we had avoided each other, and she knew nothing of my budding relationship with Jamal. I introduced them.

"Jamal, I've heard a lot about you." Susan gently took his hand and her expression lit up with a warmth I had never witnessed in her before.

The three of us sat down for chips and Coke. It amazed me how quickly Jamal opened up to Susan. There they were, laughing, joking, and carrying on like she was the big sister.

Later that night, over a twelve-pack of Coronas, I related to Susan the details of my latest interactions with Jamal, his slowly improving grades, the therapist. I told her how I had talked to all his teachers and enlisted them in our mission of getting him to his sophomore year. She beamed the whole time, and after hearing me out, she got up and gave me the biggest hug, pressing her firm braless breasts into my chest.

"You did the right thing, Matt. I'm proud of you," she said. She hugged me again, then looked up into my eyes. "You know, honey, if you weren't so fucking white I'd consider sleeping with you." She giggled with a devilish smile. I gaped at her as she opened one beer and handed me another.

"Hey," she yelled, pulling my arm, "the Pistons and Celtics are playing. Let's go to the living room."

Jealousy

Rosa shuffled her sandals into the kitchen. Though only twenty-four, by Friday night she always felt as tired as her thin hunch-backed grandmother used to look back in Brazil. She ducked her head to avoid a dangling sixty-watt light bulb, one of the bare necessities in the condensed urban apartment. Should she have beer or coffee? *Both.* She poured a full cup of heavily sugared black coffee from a metal thermos on the counter, lifted a Budweiser from the fridge, and plopped down at the small round table.

Fifteen hours earlier, at five AM, Rosa had checked in at the Marvelous Maids headquarters to pick up the daily list, directions, keys, and buckets full of cleaning gear. Like thousands of other Brazilian cleaning women in Massachusetts, Rosa put in a twelve- to fourteen-hour workday. Over the past year she had learned to read city maps and picked up the necessary vocabulary: "vacuum cleaner, laundry, mop, sweep, bleach, broom, dust, dishes, soap, sink, toilet, sponge...."

With her work-partner Sara, she had started at a downtown high-rise law office - scrubbing, scurrying, hurrying. By seven AM they moved two floors below to an accounting firm. Then they sprinted like manic robots through condos and houses of upper-middle-class residents in Beacon Hill, Back Bay, and the more suburban Brookline. At exactly noon they pulled up to a Burger King in Sara's beat-up Toyota, and on the fly munched down Whoppers and large fries. After picking up a four-pack of Red Bull at a 7-11, they raced off to the next job, Sara's eyes darting as she drove, constantly on the lookout for police cars. Getting pulled over without a driver's license could be disastrous for the two undocumented immigrants.

Rosa had not only pounded through the rigorous work schedule that day, but had also survived the regular, raw perversion that gets projected onto female cleaners, particularly those who are young and sexy. She ignored the grotesque sexual advances of the massive security guard at the downtown high-rise. She politely responded "no thank you" to the invitation of a middle-aged couple to join them in bed while she mopped their bathroom. She hid her amusement when a drunken housewife, downing one vodka and orange juice after another, ranted about her cheating husband. The fun abruptly ended though when the home-owner sent Rosa out into the back yard with the family dog – a massive German Sheppard.

"Pick it up," screamed Mrs. Lyons, throwing a plastic bag out the door at Rosa who stood in bewilderment over the dog's excrement that had fallen on the brick patio.

"What a country," Rosa later giggled to Sara as they backed out of the long driveway. "Do they expect that I'll wipe the dog's butt too?"

Call her a hick, uneducated and naïve, but her countryside upbringing provided Rosa with a sense of self that couldn't be penetrated by the toxic verbiage. And as a newly arrived immigrant she had survival instincts that formed a shield against these assaults.

Now, after a blistering week, Rosa deserved a few drinks. Tomorrow was a working day, but calmer; she had her own private cleaning gigs, receiving cash directly from the homeowners. On Saturdays she worked only a six- or seven-hour day, hitting three suburban homes on Boston's South Shore. She pulled in seventy-five dollars at each—a far better deal than the minimum wage that Marvelous Maids paid. Like all immigrant housecleaners, Rosa longed for more of her own contracts, but she felt lucky to have the three her cousin had passed on before returning to Brazil.

After finishing the coffee, Rosa took a long gulp of Budweiser and yelled, "Fachee, I need to warm my tired bones. You better leave me some hot water."

"Almost done, sweetie," responded Fatima, over the sound of the steaming shower.

A month before, when a bedroom opened up at Fatima's apartment in the Brighton neighborhood of Boston, Rosa had jumped at the invitation to move in. She had been sharing a large flat with eight Brazilian men just three blocks away. Even though the men respected Rosa, they stared at her with lonely eyes while nursing their beers after long days at construction sites. Rosa religiously kept her body completely covered, but her mere feminine presence stirred a whirlwind of testosterone throughout the house. Being the object of incalculable sexual fantasies added a layer of stress to her life that she could do without. This new situation, a two-bedroom apartment with Fatima and her boyfriend Carlos, while more expensive, gave her a priceless sense of peace and security. Plus, she and Fatima had instantly developed a warm companionship. After living in the U.S. without documents for five years, Fatima seemed to relish the opportunity to guide a younger Brazilian sister.

Invigorated by the coffee and beer Rosa pulled back her long, thick black hair and flip-flopped toward the bedroom to undress. In the hallway she threw a quick smile at a small oval mirror on the wall. Despite the long hours and physical labor, her face remained child-like and pretty. Her bright brown eyes, expressive eyebrows, full lips and smooth complexion displayed a fortuitous mix of African, European, and native Brazilian traits. In her nightly prayers she often thanked God for this bestowed beauty that had drawn compliments since her first smile as a baby.

Behind her bedroom door she lifted off her stained grey work sweatshirt and white tank top, revealing slender, muscular shoulders and arms, developed through the grueling cleaning work. She ruefully cupped her small, braless breasts. She had never regretted the year and a half of breastfeeding; those cherished moments with her daughter produced her most joyous memories. How could she forget one-year-old Diani, crawling over her body, lustily pulling up her shirt to access the milk-laden nipples? Rosa had loved how her breasts swelled with life during those months, but she'd paid a price; not only small again, they now sagged a bit. She bounced, trying to inject them with life, and then smiled at the thought of getting implants when she returned to Brazil—another dream, another few thousand dollars to earn.

Rosa pressed her hand against her stomach, proud of its flat strength, particularly since she had already given birth. Most people were shocked to hear that Rosa, who at times looked like a maturing teen, had a five-year-old daughter in Brazil. Like most Brazilian women with tight abs, Rosa made sure this part of her anatomy, adorned with a gold ring, was always exposed for public viewing, even in the midst of a New England winter. Her round, smooth bubble butt created envy in the hearts of women and stirred deep primitive tension in males. Her cousin had summed it up pretty well when he said, "Rosa, on a scale of one to ten, I'll give you an eleven for your bunda." She peeled off the skin-tight designer jeans, the everyday wear of working Brazilian females and gave her behind a tap, just to show appreciation. Completely naked, she slid into a red silk robe.

Fatima tiptoed out of the bathroom wearing one towel around her petite body and another as a turban on her head as she entered Rosa's room.

"Hey, girl, you started drinking without me?" She took her roommate's hand and led her back out to the kitchen. "Let's sit down. Have another beer before you take a shower."

At age thirty-five, with her sleek black hair and infectious smile, Fatima somehow maintained her beauty and shapely figure even though she feasted on junk food and smoked a daily pack of cigarettes. Addicted to coffee and Red Bull, she rarely missed a night of beer drinking. Fatima credited a strong work ethic as her anti-aging secret. Hailing from a culture steeped in sensuality, the seductive Brazilian used every means available to celebrate her conspicuous breasts. Push-up bras and tight, plunging shirts ensured her cleavage would attract maximum attention on her thin frame. In the summer, every so often she'd go braless in a thin, slightly see-through white halter-top and bask in the havoc this spectacle created as she jiggled through her day. Fatima endlessly bragged about a fender-bender she had caused on Tremont Street in downtown Boston the previous July. A middle-aged driver of a Volvo, who couldn't take his eyes off of Fatima's bouncing mammary glands, slammed into a BMW driven by a young foreign student. Standing on the sidewalk, Fatima howled and video-taped the chaotic confrontation that caused a major traffic jam.

"So what are we up to tonight?" asked Fatima, setting down two beers. "Do you have a date?"

"No," responded Rosa, leaning her elbows on the table.

"Good, Carlos is working. You feel like dancing?"

"Ayee, Fachee, I'm beat. Fourteen hours today, and I have to work tomorrow. What about dancing tomorrow night? Then I can sleep in all day on Sunday. Thank God for Sundays."

"Okay, I'm beat too," said Fatima, shaking her long hair. "Let's just order some food. I'll run down to the corner to get more beer."

An hour later, the kitchen table was covered with boxes of Chinese food, four empty beer cans, and a butt-filled ashtray. Lighting another cigarette, Fatima turned and rested a hand on Rosa's knee.

"My little sister, I'm dying of curiosity, but given our crazy schedules we haven't had any girl talk in ages. What's the latest?"

Rosa looked down, mildly ashamed about having two boyfriends—something she would never have dreamed of in the conservative Brazilian countryside where gossip rules. She hadn't planned this predicament, but now faced a real-life dilemma. She had met Thiago, a Brazilian painting contractor, and Bobby, an American lawyer, at different parties on the same weekend. While not yet committed to either, she found both of these men attractive. Each had a unique sense of humor, a handsome smile, and could carry on a conversation. Most refreshingly, they held their machismo in check. Phone calls led to coffees, romantic walks, flowers, wine-sipping dinners, and full-blown courtships; within a month she was sleeping with both. While Rosa hadn't directly lied, the two men still remained unaware of each other's existence.

"Ayee, Fachee, I don't know what to do. Last week Bobby came by after work. He brought some dinner for me and left at nine o'clock -- of course, after we had desert. At nine-thirty Thiago stopped by without calling. I hadn't even showered after my roll with Bobby, so I had to say I was sick. Imagine if he had arrived a half hour earlier: oh...my...God. I have to do something soon."

"Which one do you like more? Do you feel in love with one of them?"

"I'm still not sure I know what love is," said Rosa with a shrug. "But they are both nice guys — fun and romantic. I don't feel crazy in love with either yet, but I really enjoy them."

"How are they in bed? How is the American?" asked Fatima, raising an eyebrow. "You know that I've slept with a lot of Brazilian men – oh yeah, and one Colombian – but I've never been to bed with an American, so I'm curious."

Rosa blushed. "Please."

"Really, girl, how do they compare?"

"What can I say? They both have experience; they understand my body and know how to treat a woman in bed. That's all I'm going to tell you." Rosa laughed.

Fatima gave Rosa a wicked grin. "Then why not keep them both? You're not living with either."

"That's the problem," said Rosa. "I only want one man, one good man, but neither has shown any indication of making a commitment. Plus they are both still married. They tell me they are separated, and they don't wear their wedding rings — at least not in front of me — but neither has ever invited me to his house. So how the hell do I know if they are even separated?"

Fatima stood and opened the fridge. "You want another beer?"

"Sure."

"Do you ask them why they don't invite you to their houses?"

Rosa threw her head back and sighed. "The same thing — that they have their kids staying with them; that the aren't ready to meet me."

"How many kids do they have?" asked Fatima, facing Rosa and moving her chair closer.

"Thiago says he has two: a four-year-old boy and a girl who is two. Bobby says he has just one, a three-year-old daughter."

"So the only place you sleep with them is here in your bed?"

"They take me to hotels too."

"Hmm. Are they generous with you?"

"What do you mean?"

"You know what I mean. Are they helping you with your bills? Do they know you have a child in Brazil?" Fatima got up and paced the kitchen floor.

"Of course they know about Diani."

"And they haven't offered to help you with money?"

"Bobby bought me this," Rosa said defensively, running her fingers through a delicate gold necklace. "He must have paid three hundred dollars. They take me to nice restaurants."

Fatima continued circling the kitchen table, a beer in one hand, a cigarette in the other. "But girl, you don't understand. If they're getting what they want from you, whenever they want it, they need to take care of you. Rosa, you are beautiful. Do they think they can sleep with a beautiful girl whenever they feel like it and not help you out? Do you know that Carlos pays my rent, all my bills, and he does the food shopping? You know I even have him cooking most nights. He bought me my car. Do you think he'd be living with me if he didn't do this? Shit, there are twenty Brazilian men I know who would take his place in a second, and the same goes for you."

"So you're not spending any money for living expenses?" asked Rosa.

"No way. I send all the money I make cleaning to my bank account in Brazil. My father has already bought four houses for me. He's collecting rent on all of them; putting the money in the bank.

Before I go back my goal is to own seven or eight houses. Then I'll be set for life. I figure another two years. Then, thank-you America, and bye-bye." She waved her arm, leaving a trail of smoke and ash.

Rosa shook her head in wonderment. "How much is a house?"

"These days, with the exchange rate four to one, you can buy a decent house for about fifteen thousands dollars."

"After a full year here I haven't saved anything," Rosa lamented. "In fact, I still owe my cousin four thousand dollars for getting me over the border. I kill myself working seventy hours a week, but I still haven't sent a penny back home. And until I can show that I have money, a house, and a means of income, I'll never get custody of my girl." Her voice shook and a tear rolled down her cheek. "I'm so frustrated."

Fatima leaned over and softly caressed Rosa's face. "I don't want to tell you how to live your life, sweet girl, but a guy needs to take care of you; it's as simple as that."

"Fachee, I know I need money, but I also want love."

"So do I, but what's better: love with money, or love without money? Plus, if a man truly loves you he'll go crazy and work hard to make you happy. Carlos is a very good and affectionate man, but if he didn't have any earning power, there's no way he'd be living here with me. I love him, but one reason I love him is because he works hard to provide for me. Ayee, meu amor, we're out of beer. Let me run out to get another six-pack." Fatima ran her fingers through Rosa's hair and kissed her forehead.

Slightly intoxicated, Rosa sat at the table, her chin propped in open palms. After struggling in Boston for a year and aching for her daughter, she still had no regrets. Just thirteen months before in Brazil, she had been trapped in a miserable seven-year marriage with a domineering husband twice her age. When Roberto had proposed to her just before her sixteenth birthday, he offered a reality that Brazilian girls in the rural interior dreamed of: a large house, modern bathrooms, running water, plasma TVs, maids, cooks, and financial security. Instantly, she could escape her family's poverty, her mother's long daily list of chores, and caring for her younger siblings. And a marriage, she assumed, would rescue her from the virtual house arrest of her obsessively protective father, a father who had abruptly terminated her education in the fifth grade after hearing neighbors gossip that she kissed a boy on the school bus.

Shortly after an extravagant wedding, the sudden awareness that she had to fulfill a tightly prescribed role had crushed her naïve dream of finding love. Without hesitation, Roberto set up the rules: She stayed in the house unless accompanied by him; other than her immediate family, she would have no visitors (other females would only fill her head with garbage); she would raise many children; she would not look at or talk to any of his workers on the cattle ranch.

Before the marriage, her father had controlled her every move. Now that responsibility had been handed off to another male; one she was obligated to sleep with. Her first sexual experience, two nights after the wedding, resulted only in pain and disgust. Roberto just didn't have the chemical formula to stimulate her natural lubricants. She then dreaded his nightly advances, but understood her conjugal responsibilities. During those moments, she lay on her back with closed eyes, praying for him to finish so she could run to the bathroom, clean up, and go to sleep. Although seeming puzzled by the tears that sometimes rolled down her cheeks during his thrashing, Roberto never felt the need to ask about them.

It took three years for Rosa to get pregnant, and after Diani's birth the marriage further deteriorated as Rosa's attention focused exclusively on her daughter. Roberto didn't even bother to hide his sexual adventures with other women in their village, including the two young maids in the home, who received generous bonuses for accommodating his urges. Most nights Rosa escaped into the baby's room, falling asleep watching the novellas while Roberto immersed himself in beer and soccer games in the living room. Trapped on a sprawling and isolated cattle farm with a madly possessive husband, Rosa found comfort in her daughter, whom she adored with all her heart. But her freedom-seeking, love-craving soul never stopped ticking its way toward an explosion.

Long past her limit, one Sunday afternoon, with the help of two shots of Brazilian rum, Rosa informed Roberto that she wanted a divorce. He had laughed, found his own bottle of rum, and continued to laugh. Later that night in bed he expressed his contempt by violently forcing himself into her. And at the moment of his grunting, rage-filled climax, Rosa promised herself that never again would this man touch her.

The next day she boarded a bus with Diani and took the eight-hour ride to Belo Horizonte, where her parents had moved. While her mother embraced the escapees with warm, open arms, Rosa's father wrestled with an age-old conflict: the deep love of his daughter versus the rigid machismo culture. While his instincts pushed him to welcome, take in, and protect his girls, pride won the day. He demanded that they return to Roberto. Rosa had made the decision to marry, and marriage was forever, he pointed out with a resolute determination. It pained him greatly, but she had a lifelong duty to adhere to.

As Rosa stalled for a few more days, pondering the next move, her cousin called from the United States and threw down a tempting wild card. She'd loan Rosa the ten thousand dollars necessary for a coyote to get her over the Mexican border. And so Rosa found herself thinking the unthinkable: disobeying her father and abandoning her daughter.

"Come, Rosa," her cousin pleaded. "There are plenty of jobs here, and you can pay me back with no interest."

Within three weeks Rosa had relinquished custody of her daughter to Roberto. According to her carefully crafted plan, Rosa would have enough money in three years to return to Brazil, be self-sufficient, and gain back guardianship. She prayed that one day Diani would understand and forgive her. Leaving her child wrenched her guts, but she refused to look back; the thirst for freedom trumped her fervent maternal instincts. And what better gift than freedom could she offer her daughter? Roberto was a monster as a husband, but Rosa did trust him as a father. While he didn't have much capacity to love Diani, he would keep her safe and well-cared for. That was the most Rosa could expect.

No, she didn't regret the decisions that had led her to Boston. But now she did need to think more about how to secure a bountiful future. She fantasized about a comfortable home, just for her and Diani. Maybe a lover – a gentle, sensitive lover -- could occasionally come by, but what she truly wanted most was to live with her daughter in peace.

In the U.S. Rosa had to work a slave-like schedule, but she also discovered an exhilarating sense of liberty. Thrilled to make her daily life style decisions, she bounced out of bed each day, eyes wide open, bursting with energy and anticipation. Never again would she be caught in the strangling cage of machismo.

With a sexual history limited to the horror of her husband, she ached to experiment. Possessing the erotic curiosity of a sixteen-year-old, she swooned over romantic Brazilian love songs. Three consecutive short-term relationships with Brazilian men temporarily satiated her hunger. Emboldened by her cousin's graphic advice, she discovered the power of her sex and learned how to pleasure her man. She came to appreciate the joy of taking playful risks in bed and how to guide partners toward her own fulfillment. Booty call on her terms and being shameless under the covers could be fun. While each of these flings began with a burst of lust, romance, and hope, she terminated each abruptly when male dominance and possessiveness raised their ugly twin heads. For as much as she enjoyed the diversion of these adventures, she knew she would never again be squeezed into a prefabricated role. Her hyper-sensitive machismo radar had zero tolerance. "If I don't find a good man soon," she said to Sara during a coffee break, "I'm done. I'll find a woman – and I'm serious. Women are affectionate and affection is what I need."

Rosa looked up as Fatima came bouncing back into the kitchen with another six-pack, Marlboros, and Doritos.

"You know, Rosa, we should be proud of ourselves," Fatima declared, huffing as she opened two Coronas. "Look at how many Brazilian women work as go-go girls. I was talking to Fabiana — you know, the blonde girl from São Paulo? She just started working at a strip club in Rhode Island, and she's proud of it. Supposedly, she won't have sex with anyone; she's just dancing nude. But you know how that goes. She only dances for about twenty minutes each hour, and the rest of the time she's talking to men and drinking."

"It's better than being a prostitute," said Rosa, leaning back in her chair. "We all know Brazilian girls who take on dozens of men every day and have their lives destroyed. At least the go-go girls get paid just to dance and they aren't forced to have sex. This Latina girl – Cristina, that I used to clean with - she started working in a massage parlor and now the poor thing is a full-time puta."

"Ayee, but from what I know," said Fatima, taking off her leather coat and leaning against the counter, "most go-go girls end up just like prostitutes. They start drinking at the clubs, they are offered drugs, and they get lost. Maybe they begin by having sex with someone they find attractive and think, 'Wow, I can have some fun and get a hundred dollars.' Then they find themselves looking for more and more money, and soon they start having sex with any man at the club who asks for it. You know, they have disgusting bedrooms upstairs at those clubs. Say they have sex with two guys and make two hundred dollars. Then the next night they think, 'Hey, if I have sex with four guys, I can make four hundred dollars.' And I wonder if they ever save any of that money. Most likely they buy expensive clothes and jewelry, get their hair done every other day, a nice car, a fancy apartment. This is the devil's money, and nothing good can come from it."

Fatima lit another cigarette and blew a stream of smoke off to the side. "Anyway, girl, let's get back to your situation." She poked the glowing end of the Marlboro toward her friend. "Rosa, men will play us if we let them. We have to be smarter. We have to take advantage of their weaknesses — and you know what is their biggest weakness?"

"What?"

"Jealousy."

"You think so?"

"Sweetie," said Fatima, leaning in and gripping her shoulders. "All men are jealous. Girl, we women need to understand and use this force to our advantage. When a man is struck by jealousy, first he goes into a rage. Then he becomes a little boy who will do anything possible to please Mommy. At this point, Mommy needs to take control. Rosa, do both of the men have money?"

Rosa nodded. "Bobby is a lawyer and Thiago has a painting company. Bobbie has a Mercedes and Thiago drives a new truck."

"Uh huh, so they have money for sure. Girl, listen to me. I have an idea that will help you. We'll get at least one of them to respect you — maybe both."

At four o'clock on Saturday afternoon, Rosa entered the Days-Inn Motel, one arm wrapped around Thiago, the other holding a Victoria Secret gift bag. They planned to spend five hours together. Thiago claimed he couldn't sleep the night, as he needed to pick up his kids from the sitter.

"Baby," said Rosa, "I'm going to take a shower; a long shower to get all the cleaning chemicals off my body."

"That's fine, *querida*. I'll just watch the soccer game and get our drinks ready."

Rosa dropped her handbag and cell phone on the king-size bed and sauntered into the bathroom. As the hot water and steam healed her body, she belted out traditional Brazilian romance songs. *What a luxury,* she thought, *to have unlimited hot water.*

A half hour later, she strolled out of the bathroom wearing high heels and new black lace lingerie.

"Baby, you want to take a quick shower?" she asked innocently. Thiago ignored her and kept pacing the carpeted room. "Is something wrong?" asked Rosa.

Thiago stared at her with an agitation she had never before

seen in him.

"Who is Bobby?"

"What are you talking about?" she asked coyly.

"Bobby, that's who I'm talking about. Someone named Bobby keeps calling you."

"You were looking at my cell phone?" Rosa said, trying out a hint of defiance.

"Well, it kept ringing; he called three times. The phone was sitting on the bed next to me. What am I supposed to do? Not look at it? So who is Bobby?"

Rosa feigned outrage. "Bobby is a friend, okay?"

"Why is he calling you three times, and what do you mean by *friend*?"

Rosa, hands on hips, took a deep breath. "Listen, Thiago, I'm not married to you. I honestly don't know if you live with your wife, since you've never invited me to your house. So what is it to you if I have a friend?"

Thiago threw his hands into the air. "I told you, Rosa, I'm separated from my wife."

Rosa arched her brows and shrugged. "Whatever. Let's forget about it and have a nice time like we planned." Reaching up, she embraced him and kissed his neck, but he pushed her away.

"What kind of friend is Bobby? He's an American, right?"

"Yes, he's American, but he speaks Portuguese."

"Do you sleep with him?"

"Thiago, do we have to talk about this now?"

"My God, Rosa. You are not denying it. You *are* sleeping with him. Jesus Christ." He twisted away, grabbed a pillow, and slammed it down on the bed.

Rosa stepped toward him, but again he pushed her away, this time with more force.

"Rosa, I can't believe this."

"Look, Thiago, I only see you for a few hours each week. Do you think you can control my life?"

"Let's go," he said, putting on his shoes.

"Where?"

"I'm leaving. You want a ride home?"

"Give me a minute."

Rosa quickly dressed into her street clothes and then remained silent in the car until they pulled up to the front of her apartment.

"Thiago, you're acting like a child," she said as she opened the car door.

"Just go, Rosa, go." He slammed the door behind her and sped off.

Rosa sprawled on the living room couch, smiling, fascinated by Fatima's wisdom. She began dancing in front of the mirror to some loud Brazilian country music, but turned it down quickly when her phone lit up.

"Who is Thiago?" Bobby demanded.

"Hello to you to," she said, as if taken aback. "Why are you asking?"

"Because he just called me to tell me how he has sex with you every day. He told me the details of things you like in bed – and he's right."

"Ayee, he's crazy, Bobby. Yes, I've been dating him casually every once in a while, but it's nothing serious. And I certainly don't see him every day."

"How did he get my number?"

"I don't know. Maybe he found it in my cell phone. Brazilian men are always going through women's phones."

"Well, thanks for telling me about him," Bobby said. "Thanks for letting me have to deal with a nut. What's next? He's going to start stalking me? How many more boyfriends do you have?"

"I don't feel like talking now. I'll call you later." Rosa grinned as she hung up.

During the next two weeks, Rosa had little time alone. She engaged in numerous impassioned conversations with her two suitors: over the phone, sitting in cars, restaurants, coffee shops, and walking in parks. Both Bobby and Thiago expressed rage, shed tears, took her to malls, bought her gifts, confessed undying love, and made financial promises that were perhaps unwise, given that they both had responsibilities to their wives and children.

"So, girl," said Fatima, when the friends finally had a chance to commiserate at the kitchen table. "I know something is up, but give me all the details."

"Ayee, Fachee, you and your tricks. You have no idea how crazy these last few weeks have been."

"So which one are you with?"

"I'm seeing a lot of Bobby, but I'm still talking to Thiago." Rosa giggled, sipping her coffee.

"What happened?"

"Let's see, where to start," said Rosa, beaming. "First of all, Thiago confessed to me that he still lives with his wife and kids, but supposedly he is going to move out and get his own place next month. He says I'm the love of his life and he'll get a divorce. I did what you said. I told him I needed ten thousand dollars because I wanted to buy a home in Brazil to provide security for my daughter. And guess what? Within two days, he gave me half and said he'd get the rest in two weeks. I had to try really hard not to look as shocked as I felt. Your plan worked!"

Fatima smirked and blew a smoke ring. "What did I tell you? You're worth every penny."

"And then there's Bobby. He proved to me that he is truly separated from his wife by finally inviting me to his apartment. It's so cozy and relaxing there—so much better than the hotel. Anyway, when I explained to him about the ten thousand dollars he told me that he wanted to help me, but he couldn't right now. I ignored all his calls for a few days, and then he left me a message saying he took a loan. Last week he gave me the full amount. Ayee, Fachee, I paid off my cousin and I wired the rest to my father so he can start looking for a deal on a house. He's so happy for me, and I feel like I'm finally out of my financial hole. I've got some momentum now, and if I can get two more houses set, I think I can return to Brazil and get at least joint custody of my daughter."

"So you haven't made a commitment to either guy?"

"No, not yet. I'm leaning towards Bobby. He is the most available, since he is now legally separated and has his own place. And he went out on a limb for me with that loan, so I know he's serious."

"What are you going to do next?"

"I don't know. But I like where I'm at right now."

"Girl, you're learning," said Fatima, giving her a high five.

Rosa glanced at her vibrating cell phone. Thiago's name leaped off the screen.

Manhood

Tito entered the first floor apartment, cautiously closed the door, and tiptoed through the hallway. He peeked into the kitchen and saw his shirtless uncle sipping coffee, engrossed in the *Boston Herald* tabloid spread out on the table. Taking a deep breath, Tito continued moving stealthily towards his bedroom.

"Tito, ven'ca."

"Shit," muttered the fourteen-year-old as he sauntered back, his baggy jeans falling over black and white Reeboks.

"Como estas?" asked Marco, seeking his nephew's large brown eyes.

"Okay," he answered, sucking his lower lip to erase the blood traces.

"Look at me," boomed Marco.

Tito raised his head and clenched his jaw. Marco leapt out of his chair and landed his massive hands on the boy's shoulders. He narrowed his eyes and his nostrils flared at the sight of Tito's swollen split lip.

"Not again. They did it again?"

"Yes," nodded Tito.

"They hit you in the mouth?"

"One of them backhanded me."

"What did they take this time?"

"Eight dollars and my bus pass."

"Jesus Christ, that's it." Marco pounded his fist on the table. "We're going to solve this problem now, right now."

The vein above his uncle's left eye throbbed and his contorted face turned cherry red. Thirty-six years old with a shaved head, Marco maintained a youthful six-foot physique by pumping iron in the gym three to four times a week. His gang-themed tattoos and scarred-up face provided graphic reminders of his upbringing in Spanish Harlem.

"Goddamn it; we're going out there," said Marco as he pulled on a white muscle T-shirt. He stormed into the hallway and returned gripping a thirty-four-inch metal baseball bat. "Come on, Tito. Let's go deal with these punks."

Tito winced. On most summer days Marco used the bat to hit easy fly balls to his six-year-old twin sons at the baseball diamond across the street. But now he held the slugger as a deadly club.

Marco's wife Sonia, aroused from breast-feeding in the bedroom, rushed into the kitchen, clutching her wide-eyed eight-month-old daughter. "Dios mio, Marco. Que pasa?"

"Sonia, stay out of this. This is the third time these maggots have messed with him. Three strikes and they're out."

Marco wrapped his hands around the bat, the veins in his forearms and biceps pulsating with adrenaline-rich blood. "Let's go, Tito. I'm going to show you street justice."

Tito slowly moved forward, but Sonia pushed him back toward the kitchen table. "Sit down," she commanded. She turned to Marco. "Por amor de Dios. Think for a minute. You are not a street thug anymore; you are a father." She shoved the baby into Marco's arms, but he refused to drop the bat to take her. Sonia scampered to the living room and plunked the girl down in the playpen. Then the petite Latina rushed her husband, grabbed the bat, and tore it out of his grip.

Tito hung back, shocked by her ferocity; Sonia had always been the sweetest and calmest of his many aunts.

"For Christ's sake, we are going to think about this, not charge out into the street like animals," Sonia demanded. "I've already lost a brother to this stupidity, and it won't happen again." She looked out to the living room, where a photo of her young brother hung on the wall. Luis, the overwhelming family favorite with his playful nature and good looks, had been stabbed to death in New York five years before. Sonia and her mother had dressed in black for an entire year after the shocking tragedy.

"Give me the bat," warned Marco, his voice shaking as he cornered her.

"Never," she fired back.

Marco overpowered her and took possession of the weapon. Yanking on Tito's shirt, he stomped towards the door.

"No," screamed Sonia, grabbing her husband's knees from behind.

The baby wailed from the living room as, like a bulldozing fullback, Marco broke the tackle and stumbled out onto the sidewalk. He began trotting towards Washington Street, pulling Tito at his side. Sonia bolted out the front door behind them. An athlete in high school, she sprinted barefoot on the asphalt until she maneuvered in front of her husband, forcing him to halt on the sidewalk.

"Marco Torres, listen to me," she wailed, pulling his T-shirt strap. "You are a Boston fireman. You are supposed to fight fires. You cannot be fighting in the street. You are a fireman, Marco. Marco, por favor." She fell sobbing at his feet, locking her wrists around his ankles.

By now, over a dozen neighbors had appeared on their front stoops, drawn from their televisions to the real-time urban drama. Marco glanced down at his wife and then looked ahead to the intersection two blocks away, where a group of male teens loitered about in front of the corner convenience store. Some leaned on the hood of a low-riding black Honda that had pulled to the curb. The thumping bass of a reggaeton beat projected from the car windows. Marco wiped the sweat on his forehead and took several deep breaths while Tito waited anxiously.

"Baby, you're right," he finally said, helping Sonia to her feet as her sobs simmered to whimpers. "I'm sorry." He held her tightly, and she buried her face in his chest.

"I don't want to lose you, Marco. I don't want to-to lose T-tito," she stammered.

Then in silence, with Sonia carrying the bat and Marco draping his arm over Tito's shoulder, they headed back to the house, and the neighbors returned to their televisions. Marco sat on the front stoop and Sonia continued feeding the baby.

In his bedroom Tito lost himself in Nintendo, in a world where he had some control, where he had a chance of defeating the enemy. A freshman at nearby Roosevelt High School, Tito had fallen into the whirlpool of adolescence, barely keeping afloat. He had moved in with Marco, Sonia, their twin boys, and baby daughter after his parents separated six months before. Tito's mother, Maria — Marco's sister — had retreated to Puerto Rico shortly after the breakup and planned on a return to Boston in a year. Tito's father had moved to Brooklyn, where he was living with an undocumented Colombian woman and her three kids. Tito desperately missed his mother, but had very little to say when she called; he hadn't heard from his father in months. His younger cousins could be fun, but most often they were a bother. He felt Sonia's radiating warmth, but the baby demanded most of her attention. He found Marco's constant commands and unsolicited advice intimidating and he delighted in the peaceful interludes when his uncle slept at the firehouse.

At Roosevelt High, Tito maintained a semi-anonymous profile. Not quite an outcast or a nerd, he drifted on the outermost fringes of one of the popular athletic cliques. An older cousin, Javier, was a leader in this group, and he had his young relative's back. While Tito's affiliation with Javier didn't buy him popularity, it did provide a measure of safety and protection within the institutional walls. But Tito hadn't found his stride; he didn't have a voice in the complex web of social networks at the dysfunctional high school. He doodled or dozed through most of his classes, and only one teacher even tried to engage him. Tito did the minimum to maintain a D+ average but no one pushed him; no one had laid out a motivating vision. Life consisted mostly of sleepwalking through school, Nintendo, computer games, and TV.

Family parties on weekends provided some diversion and relief from the weekly monotony. Within Tito's extended Latino family, excuses for parties sprouted up regularly: birthdays, baptisms, confirmations, graduations, first communions, quinceañeras, and engagements. During these occasions, Tito studied Female Anatomy 101 with some of his cousins and their friends through kissing games, wrestling, dirty dancing, and wild touching in the dark, where he had learned how to wet his fingers. These secretive, short-lived adventures provided enough thrills to feed his budding fantasies, but Tito hadn't yet figured out how to even begin the intricacies of dating.

Lying in bed later that night, Tito did not go into his usual fantasy mode. Instead, his mind raced as he imagined the various street scenes that could have played out if not for Sonia's intervention. Then he heard his uncle and aunt conversing in their bedroom across the hallway.

"I'm sorry, baby," said Marco. "I haven't gone street ballistic like that in years. I can't believe I almost got pulled into that zone. God, all those years dreaming of being a firefighter . . . it all could have been lost in an instant."

"Ayee, Marco," Sonia responded. "I couldn't let you loose on that corner with a bat. You can't be teaching Tito that stuff."

"But baby, what is the answer? Those punks are humiliating Tito every day."

"I know. I wish we could go to the police, but that's useless."

"You were right to stop me, baby. But it's so frustrating. I'm still pissed off."

"Mi amor, those kids are lost. They are filled with rage and have no fear. What they do have is guns, though, and you know the slightest word could get you or our nephew shot."

Marco grunted but didn't reply.

"Still, Marco, we can't fight hate with hate. We have to rise above them. We'll never win with violence. Imagine if you beat up some of them. They know where we live. Our kids, us — we'd never be safe in our own home."

"But Sonia, what do I do? We can't move; we just bought this house. I want to teach Tito how to be a man, but how does a man handle this situation?"

"Let's just stay cool. Tell Tito to walk home by a different route, so he doesn't have to pass them. Trust in God, mi amor. Please promise me you won't mess with those kids. I find you more a man, my love, when you use your mind, not your fists. You're an intelligent man. Please promise."

"Okay, I promise baby," Marco replied.

The light clicked and the bed creaked and rustled. "Dulces sueños," whispered Sonia.

Tito, too, burrowed into his pillow, feeling relieved. His uncle's macho stance had terrified him, and he marveled at how his aunt Sonia's calm grace brought a deeper level of understanding to this enigma. As he drifted off to sleep, he felt the secure embrace of Sonia's wisdom filling him with an unexpected new strength.

The next day at the fire station, Marco warmly embraced Jonathan, his closest co-worker.

"Yo Marco," said Jonathan, "my uncle Willie just called. You know, the plumber. He's looking for a teen to help him — afternoons and weekends. Think your nephew would be interested?"

In a flash, Marco visualized Tito sitting in front of the Nintendo box and gave Willie a call.

Self-employed, Willie Johnson had learned the plumber's trade from his grandfather and father. "If you're a friend of Jon's, then I'm sure we can work something out," he told Marco in an upbeat tone.

That evening, when Marco first ran the idea by Tito, the boy responded, "I don't think so" without looking up from his video game. But Sonia's tranquil yet forceful urging convinced Tito to accept a weeklong trial period.

A man of habit and ritual, Willie had a late lunch every day at a café just a few train stops from Roosevelt High. Tito agreed to meet him there and then work from 2:30 to 6:30 each afternoon. A towering black man with massive arms and shoulders, Willie had passed his seventieth birthday, but he looked closer to fifty. His short Afro and beard were speckled evenly with black and white. He wore the old-time denim overalls and tattered construction boots. Willie walked with a limp from an old high school football injury and needed to wear a back support, but overall he maintained a robust health that matched his resonant voice. Immediately Tito felt the warm aura of this gentle giant.

During the first week they worked on a bathroom in the basement of a single-family home, installing a sink, shower, and toilet. As Tito served as an all-purpose assistant, fetching tools and parts, Willie took time to carefully explain each step. Tito quickly tuned in to Willie's patient tutelage and uncovered a novel pleasure in comprehending the basics of the trade.

On Friday, after finishing the job, they fought the rush hour traffic in Willie's battered pick-up. After down-shifting for a red light, Willie took a healthy swig of Jack Daniel's he had pulled from under his seat. He leaned back and grinned.

"Your uncle said you would try working for a week. So what do you think?"

"I think I like it," said Tito, looking unsuccessfully for a seatbelt.

Willie gave a satisfied nod. "You're a good worker. You know, Tito, I like having a young partner on the job. It keeps me going. I think you'll work out fine. I like the way you listen, your focus. About twenty years ago my son used to join me after school — the same schedule as you."

"Is he a plumber now?"

Willie shook his head and sighed as he barreled along, shifting into second gear on Columbia Road. "No; unfortunately he's no longer with us. When he was sixteen, his mama passed away and he was angry — started running with the wrong crowd. One night I got a call to identify his body. He'd been jumped by some kids from another street - stabbed him to death. Seems he had a feud going."

Willie turned and met Tito's wide eyes. "Yeah, for a year, I was numb — just destroyed; nothing is worse in life than losing a child. I couldn't even work. Luckily my brother and his wife looked after me. Finally I somehow found strength — had to be the Lord — and I realized that my only satisfaction in life would come from working and passing on my craft to the next generation. So over the years I've always had a kid like yourself working with me. The last helper I had just went off to college last month."

Willie nodded with pride as he fumbled with his pipe and lighter. "I hope you'll study and go off to college too, Tito, but no matter what you do, plumbing can come in real handy in life. You can work part-time and pay your tuition. I may be old school, but I truly believe that every young man should learn a trade — even if they go to college. You can always fall back on plumbing; there'll always be a need for us."

"I like it. I like it a lot," confirmed Tito, enjoying the scent of the tobacco. "And you're a good teacher."

Willie beamed and reached down to find the Jack.

From that day on, Tito rushed out of school every afternoon to the subway station. He eagerly jumped out of bed early on Saturday mornings. Weeks went by, then months. He enjoyed the new construction, renovations, and repairs, but his favorite jobs were the emergency calls with the mystery leaks. Sometimes the solution would be obvious as soon as they entered a house: a burst pipe, a puddle under a water heater. But other times they'd be baffled, and Willie would go into his Sherlock Holmes deductive mode, sunk deep in thought, articulating his thought process as a fascinated Tito anxiously awaited the conclusion. "Water always takes the easiest route down," Willie would say, stroking his beard in the flooded basement of a triple-decker or the cramped bedroom of a sixth-floor apartment. Then they'd have to open a wall, a ceiling, or drill through a floor in order to find the root cause—a worn O-ring on a valve, a blown-out thermostat, a clogged drain, a dirt-filled sump pump.

Tito spent each workday with intense engagement, and his plumbing IQ rocketed. Fascinated by the functioning of a toilet, he came to understand the adjustments and relationships between the gasket, flush ball, flapper, and tank lever. He learned where and how drainage blockages occur and how to unclog them. He inquired about the differences between cast iron, copper, brass, stainless steel, and PVC. Each day he felt more familiar with the tools and the variety of parts: washers, O-rings, drain tubes, crosses, tees, stop valves, flanges, slip joints, clamps. The sexual connotations of some plumbing parts amused him: male adapters, female adapters, cocks, nuts, couplings, bushings, and nipples.

"Yeah, plumbers are a perverted bunch," laughed Willie.

For about a month they worked on a massive Dorchester one-family. A leading black banker in Boston had purchased the property with the goal of making it the ultimate urban dream house for his wife and two young daughters. The huge Victorian with an attached barn sat on an acre of land and had been completely gutted. An army of black contractors had been hired: electricians, carpenters, air conditioning specialists, landscapers, painters, floor sanders, roofers, gutter hangers, siding appliers, framers, sheet-rockers, and masons. Each day a bright, bellowing brotherhood fanned out through the three floors, attic, and basement. They never seemed to be in a hurry, but worked steadily, and throughout the day incessant jokes rocked through the structure. The black workers greeted the one Puerto Rican electrician with "Hey, Goya man."

"What's up, Aunt Jemima?" he'd respond, taking it up another notch.

"Hey amigo, I went out with a Puerto Rican chick last night. She told me she needed a black man to do her right."

"Yeah, I saw you with her; the one that weighs about three hundred pounds. You're lucky she didn't suffocate you. Are those her little hairs there stuck between your teeth?"

And like that, they'd banter away.

One blustery November day as they sat with their backs against the sunny side of the barn, Willie poured Tito a strong cup of coffee from his thermos.

"So Willie, why do you like plumbing so much?" asked Tito.

Willie narrowed his slightly bloodshot eyes. "Hmmm, Tito, you're right. I love plumbing. And I can tell you why. First of all, I come from a long line of craftsmen from the Deep South. I have cousins, nephews and grandchildren all over Boston running small construction companies. And plumbing is the link to my grandfather and father. Every time I think about how to solve a problem, my grandfather and father are right there with me. We spent so many years together, the three of us, that it's like they never left. I swear they put thoughts into my mind when I need a solution, when I need to fix something I can't figure out. It's almost like they was standing beside me in the flesh and blood.

"The other reason," the old man continued, "is because we're needed. We're important, us plumbers. Think about it—we control the very source of life. No one can live without water. Our job is to make sure the water comes in—nice, neat, and clean. We set up the system so the water can do its job while it's in the house and so it leaves as quietly as it came in. So we're controlling the flow of life."

Willie paused, but Tito just sipped at his coffee and nodded for him to continue.

"Humans use water to drink, cook, clean our bodies, to heat our homes, wash dishes and clothes, to stay healthy, to get rid of our own waste. Plumbers need to make sure it doesn't leak or get clogged up, and we need to make sure we maintain the pressure so it reaches the higher floors of those apartment buildings. We keep the water cold for drinking and hot for taking a shower. Not one of these homes would be livable without good plumbing. They say that most human beings would die in about three days without water, so I see this as a very sacred responsibility. This is what I love about my job, and I only ask that God keep me healthy for another ten years or so."

Willie raised his eyes skyward and nodded firmly.

After six months with Willie, Tito found his power of concentration stronger. He now tuned into his teachers at the high school — at least the ones who weren't painfully boring. Mathematics became a welcome challenge — something he could see had practical applications, from measuring the length and angles of pipes to calculating water pressure. He grew to appreciate the internal rewards of solving difficult math problems and understood the utilization of deductive reasoning.

Even better, he no longer felt awkward walking in the school corridors. Accustomed to bantering with the workmen and homeowners he met on job sites, he also talked more easily to classmates. He had long, animated conversations with his mother on the phone twice a week.

Best of all, phone calls, instant messages, and texts flowed in each night from girls in his classes. Turning wrenches, hauling pipe, drilling holes, breaking concrete, and digging had strengthened and built up Tito's hands, arms, and shoulders. The exercise complemented his adolescent transformation, and he admired his developing body in the mirror when he came out of the shower.

Despite his growing confidence, though, he continued to avoid the corner where the gang hung out, and he still had mini panic-attacks whenever he thought of their menacing presence. During one of their coffee breaks by the barn, he shared his worries with the wise elder.

"They used to take my money, threaten me, beat on me," Tito explained, "but now I take another route to get home. It's longer, but at least I don't have to pass by their corner."

Sitting up against a tree stump, Willie took a long gulp of coffee from his thermos cup.

"That's good, Tito," he said. "It's always best to avoid conflicts. You need to think like a strategist, just like we do when we go out on an emergency call. Believe me, I've thought a lot about all this violence and chaos ever since my boy was killed. These days a young man needs to understand why conflicts escalate and how to prevent them. We have to outwit and outmaneuver the negative forces so we're not drawn into a downward vortex. Tell me, why do you think this particular gang harasses you?"

Tito shrugged, sitting on the lawn with his arms wrapped around his knees. "Not sure. They said I was walking through their turf."

"Exactly," said Willie, pouring more coffee. "You know, we are an evolving species, us humans. We still have our animal instincts, but we also have a spiritual nature, an impulse to love and care for our brothers and sisters, a connection to each other and to our creator. Now those kids on the corner don't understand that they have a choice between acting on lower instincts or on higher spiritual impulses. Most animals instinctively create their own space or turf, mark it off, and guard it—just what these kids are doing. They pick on others when they're all together in a pack, to show they're big dogs. Their emotional plumbing is a mess; all sorts of blockages, pollution, frozen valves. You have to avoid getting clogged up yourself and being dragged down to their level."

"Yeah, but how do I do that?" Tito asked.

"Your first option is to deescalate the conflict. We have to control our lower instincts that tell us to escalate—to fight back. When a person faces hostility and reacts with aggression, the tensions increase. You've seen it—the situation heats up, emotions cross a certain threshold, and violence is inevitable. This is how we get into the horrific situations like the one that killed my son, like the ones that lead the TV news each night. You need to practice de-escalation skills; when you master these skills, you can walk in peace."

"Deescalate—you mean like I just don't react when they push me?"

"Right, or you can make a joke or find some other way to defuse the situation. But if you can't deescalate and you're threatened, your first choice is to escape." Willie grinned at Tito's open mouth. "Yes, son, *run*. Best way to avoid a fight. If you can't run, if you're cornered or surrounded, of course you may have to use force. But if you are strategic and smart, under most circumstances you can avoid violence. With words they will challenge your manhood. But words are just hot air. Don't give them the power to define who you are. You can create yourself. They know nothing about manhood; they are angry, insecure children in men's bodies."

Willie's soft but powerful words, "you can create yourself," found a comfortable position on the altar of Tito's mind.

Tito appreciated the mechanical and engineering aspects of plumbing, and he also began to see the art; how each problem offered a variety of solutions. With Willie's permission he took home leftover PCV pipe cuttings, elbows, and extensions. He created a simple irrigation system for Sonia's flower garden using collected rainwater and a timer he connected to an old water pump. This delighted Sonia, and her plants flourished.

At a sporting goods store, Tito noticed that expensive soccer goalposts were made out of plastic material similar to the PCV pipe. With large scraps of the pipe and some netting material he purchased, Tito astonished himself and his relatives by designing and constructing two soccer goalposts. He enlisted his younger cousins to help carry them across the street to the far end of the baseball field, where he set them up. The three played for hours, delighted with the new equipment, which soon became a magnet for the neighborhood kids. The lights at the field stayed on till 11:00 PM, so most nights Tito spent hours running, dribbling, and firing the soccer ball into the goal. He fantasized about collecting more and more pipe and creating sets of goalposts to place in parks throughout the city.

While these creative outbursts were indicative of Tito's inner transformation, the kids on the corner remained stagnant. Everyone in the neighborhood knew who they were—that all had dropped out of high school and several had been arrested for assault and battery, drug trafficking, B&E, and shoplifting. For most, since it was their first offense, they did only the six-to-twelve-month initiation in the Suffolk County House of Correction, which housed thousands of young black and Latino males. One of the gang leaders, Maximo, had been shot to death in a tenement doorway at a nearby public housing development. In spite of its collective setbacks, the group remained a force and continued their intimidating presence. The owner of the corner convenience store paid them several hundred extorted dollars each month, buying safety for himself, his family, and his employees.

On an early Saturday evening, Tito came out of the subway and headed home after a full ten-hour day. He welcomed the cool autumn breeze. For over a year he had avoided the corner. But on this particular night, he made a spontaneous decision to walk by.

"Hey, look who's here," smirked Oscar.

Tony, the largest of the crew, stepped out on the sidewalk, blocking Tito's path.

"My man, you got some cash on you? I'm the toll collector." He laughed, poking his finger into Tito's chest.

"Yeah, I've got a few bucks," said Tito, taking a step back and meeting Tony's eyes. Then he continued: "Tony, I've never done a thing to you, and you know that you don't need the few dollars I have in my pocket. I'm not looking for trouble with you guys. I'm just walking home. If it bothers you that I walk by, I can take another route."

Tony and his three companions hesitated and gaped. Here was a standoff of the strangest kind. Tito wasn't directly challenging them. He had simply requested to pass by in peace.

Tito wondered if he should run; given his many recent hours on the soccer field, he knew that none of them had a chance to catch him. Tony stepped to the side and said, "Okay, punk, I don't want your chump change anyway. But you watch your back walking around here. You got that?"

"Tony, chill," said Chino. "He's cool. He ain't down with any other crew."

Tony moved out of the way.

Tito looked behind him, made eye contact with all, nodded politely, and continued up the sidewalk. When he approached home, he noticed Marco sitting on the front steps with his arm slung around Sonia, who was rocking the baby. The twins were playing soccer across the street and Sonia's garden was filled with the bright colors of fall mums. As he opened the walkway gate, Tito exchanged smiles with the couple and the baby cooed a welcome to her older cousin.

"Hi, Tito," said Sonia.

"Hey."

"Tito, don't you usually come from the other direction?" asked Marco, frowning with concern.

"Usually, yeah, but today I thought I'd walk by the corner and see how the boys were doing."

"Aieee. Did they give you a hard time?" Sonia asked.

"They started to," said Tito, "but I let them know I wasn't looking for trouble and they backed off."

"You think it's a good idea to walk by there?" said Marco.

"Nah, I'll probably keep coming from the other direction. There's no sense in looking for problems."

"Sounds right," said Sonia. "Hey Tito, come over here." She ran her hand over his shoulders and biceps. "You're really getting strong, boy."

"Yeah, he's becoming a man," said Marco, throwing a soft punch to his chest.

"Uh huh," said Sonia as she leaned over and kissed her husband.

Don't Mess With Tanya!

To know Tanya was to know that she didn't take bullshit from anyone: no how, no way. She didn't start trouble, but look out if she was wronged. For as long as her family could remember, Tanya had always been Tanya. At the age of three she pushed five-year-old cousin Lisa off the front porch onto the sidewalk while fighting over a Barbie doll. Lisa somehow survived the six-foot fall with only bruises and scratches while learning an important lesson about dealing with her upstairs relative.

When visiting her folks in Georgia, nine-year-old Tanya delicately stuck pieces of well-chewed Bazooka bubblegum into the thick hair of her cousin Willie while he slept. This occurred several hours after he had tackled her from behind at the riverbank, causing Tanya to fall face first into several inches of cesspool-like mud. At the age of fourteen, Tanya was leisurely walking home from school with neighbor Reginald Jones on a nippy November afternoon. With Tanya's coat wide open, exposing her tight white turtleneck, young Reggie lost control of his hands and aggressively probed Tanya's well-developed chest. This spontaneous expression of endearment was met by a sucker punch that drew blood and left a scar on Tanya's knuckle, a lifelong reminder of Reginald's impropriety.

Now Tanya wasn't one of those in-your-face, cranky, rude, crass, obnoxious, mean-spirited hood rats. In fact, most of her acquaintances described her as cheerful, gracious, and charming. But she did possess her own innate sense of justice. Maybe in a previous life she had been a judge who ruled under Hammurabi's code: "An eye for an eye." Tanya's ethical views were acutely clear and simple:

"Don't mess with me, and I don't mess with you;" "Respect me and I'll respect you." And there was one more: "You start something with me; well, I'll just have to finish it." Tanya hadn't ever consciously constructed this moral stance; she figured if she'd already been like that since age three, it must be just engrained into her being.

As she developed from a tomboy into a voluptuous young woman — a stunning mixture of the Deep South and the West Indies — Tanya learned that good looks are both a blessing and a curse. In order to maintain her dignity, she had to be on alert and constantly ready for battle. At her high school she was widely respected, even though her bright smile, her full, sexy lips, her hot-chocolate skin, her halo of wild ringlets, and her artfully curved body inspired the dreams and fantasies of countless classmates. On the street, she welcomed a polite compliment, but met any verbal molestation with a toe-to-toe confrontation. As Tanya reached her late teens she received increasingly less harassment on Boston's streets, maybe because of her strong vibe, or maybe because her striking beauty raised the consciousness of her male admirers out of the gutter into a more aesthetic realm. Or maybe both.

Even though Boston's streets and schools still oozed of racial tension, Tanya was one of those unique sisters who crossed barriers of race and culture with grace. Within her urban school community she moved seamlessly into and through the cliques of African Americans, Jamaicans, Cape Verdeans, Africans, Latinos, and Asians, whether she was at a dance, in the corridors, in the cafeteria, or at a football game. Unlike her older half-sister Susan who spent her high school years bullying and terrorizing uppity white girls, Tanya actually liked some Caucasian folks. She had spent two years of middle school in the Metco Program, which bused urban kids out to suburban schools. There she had been invited to sleepovers at those huge colonial houses, where dads give rides in minivans in between raking leaves and golfing, and moms throw together quick breakfasts before heading out to yoga classes. Tanya even forgave a suburban mom who admitted she was terrified of getting car-jacked as they drove down Blue Hill Ave. on an early Sunday morning after a slumber party.

"Don't worry, there's just crack-heads and ho's out here this early," laughed Tanya as Mrs. Donnolly bit her lip, re-checked the door locks and twitched her neck at a red light.

So Tanya didn't carry an anti-white attitude, and she wasn't a man-hater, but during sophomore year, Mr. Gerrity, her social studies teacher, crossed the line onto her path of justice. In the weeks leading up to this confrontation, Tanya had great difficulty sleeping. Her mind replayed images of Gerrity's hateful looks towards his non-white students and his demeaning statements that began with "you people." Her stomach burned when he railed on a regular basis against affirmative action. Why was he always spouting about how desegregation had destroyed the Boston Public Schools? The minimal positive energy he had was reserved for the white and Asian kids who sat in front. Tanya would lose her appetite, and she often had pulsating headaches coming out of his class after absorbing his daily hate.

The climax came on the day Tanya heard Gerrity mumble the word "animals" when a group of boisterous black students passed him in the hallway. She pinned the aging white educator by his shoulders up against a row of lockers, then pushed her nose inches from his face, getting so close that she could smell the whiskey on his breath that the Tic-Tacs couldn't cover up. "Don't you ever call us animals again or I'll tear your eyeballs out," she hissed, displaying her well-manicured, but fierce nails.

Over fifty students in the hallway witnessed the assault and the story broke the record for the speed with which it rocketed through the campus – faster than the one about the freshman soccer star impregnated by a young substitute gym teacher, and faster than the one about the female vampire wannabee who had actually sucked blood out of two boys' necks. It seemed that for at least an hour everyone in the school had an opinion on Tanya's act: "Bitch don't mess," "She fucking jacked him up," "Put the cracker in his place", "She my home girl."

While this profile in courage earned Tanya rock-star status among her classmates and liberal faculty members, she ended up being suspended for five days and transferred to another class. Tanya's mother said not a word when the suspension came down, as she couldn't figure out if she was more angry or proud. Tanya's father called in from Detroit, saying, "Girl, I'm backing you up one hundred and fifty percent. If this racist son-of-a-bitch says one more word to you, I'm flying out to Boston to personally take care of whitey." To her satisfaction, Gerrity was encouraged to retire at the end of the school year; this dinosaur needed to be booted into extinction.

No, Tanya hadn't taken any bullshit in high school, and she wasn't about to take it out in the real world after she graduated. So when an elderly white owner of a clothing store began following her around while she was shopping during her lunch break, Tanya felt the blood rushing to her cheeks, her heart pounding, and a pulsing tension in the back of her neck.

"This chump is getting on my nerves," she said to Jada, a Jamaican friend and co-worker at a nursing home located in a predominantly white middle-class neighborhood on the outskirts of Boston.

"Come on, girl, let's get out of here," said Jada. "We need to be back to work in ten minutes anyway."

"Hold on a minute," said Tanya. Initially she had been disturbed by the behavior of this slight man in suspenders, who did not feel the need to be discrete about staring at the two ebony females as they examined the shoe display. But she soon accelerated to a steaming fury when, as the girls moved from aisle to aisle, the shameless shopkeeper followed them with a tired, dreary countenance.

"This sucker needs to back off. There must be fifteen people in this store and look who he's watching," Tanya whispered to Jada. "Can't two hardworking girls go to a goddamn store without being harassed by this redneck son-of-a-bitch?"

Tanya grabbed a pair of shoes and slammed them back into the display bin. She spun around and faced the storeowner. "What are you looking at?"

The aging proprietor stood motionless and continued staring.

"What are you, fucking deaf?" said Tanya, loudly enough so that several elderly white women in nearby aisles turned around with mouths open.

Jada grabbed Tanya's arm and pulled her toward the exit door.

"Calm down, girl," said Jada as they stepped out onto the sidewalk, "and stop being the angry black woman. You're about to get us arrested." Then she giggled. "I thought those old white biddies might have a heart attack."

Being led by Jada back to the nursing home, Tanya barely heard her friend's words. She smiled as she considered a perfect scheme. *Payback is a bitch.*

Anthony Dimasi had followed the path of the American Dream since his arrival in the U.S. from a small village in Italy six decades before. At the age of ten he had immigrated to Boston's North End and moved into a three-room flat with his parents, two brothers and a sister.

Ridiculed by his classmates for his inability to speak English, Tony had toughened up quickly after an Irish kid, Billy McDonough, punched him in the stomach just for a laugh. When Billy tried to trip him in the stairway the next day after recess though, Tony stabbed him in the thigh with his pencil. As the school nurse removed the lead from Billy's leg, word spread throughout the school to stay away from this crazed Italian kid. Freed from the bullies, Tony learned English with ease and established himself as an honor roll student.

Meanwhile his family had embarked on a retail clothing business that was providing a stable income. As an adult, Tony was more than surprised to learn that his father and uncle, in the early days of the business, would often buy whole truckloads of new clothes at ridiculously low prices — merchandise that had been stolen from New

York City's garment district warehouses, part of a well-organized racket. Of course, the local Boston police had to be compensated for ignoring these midnight deliveries of leather coats, designer jeans, and imported Italian shoes. But those types of deals helped to jump-start the business.

At the age of thirteen, Tony began his initiation into the clothing business and gradually picked up the essential skills of sales, store design, bookkeeping, marketing, purchasing, and most importantly, earning the satisfaction and loyalty of his customers. As Tony's family prospered, they decided to move their home and business out of the crowded North End to an outlying middle-class neighborhood within the city limits. There, the predominantly lace-curtain Irish seemed to tolerate a moderate influx of Italian, Greek, and Lebanese families, as long as they mowed their lawns and kept their sex-hungry sons away from the lily-white Catholic girls.

The clothing store flourished in a neighborhood where the hard-working and upwardly mobile locals had a lot more disposable cash in their wallets. After graduating from high school, Tony took the reins of the family establishment and married his sweetheart, Angelica, who became not only his wife, but also his lifelong business partner. Tony and Angelica's three children grew up in the store, playing hopscotch on the sidewalk, eating pizza at Mario's next door, watching TV in the backroom, and playing countless hours of hide-and-seek in the clothes racks.

In time, the Florence Clothing Store became an institution in the community. Middle-class working mothers went to the Florence for a new dress or a tight cleavage-revealing top when they needed to seduce their beer-drinking, testosterone-decreasing husbands away from the Red Sox and into the bedroom. Catholic parents ordered hundreds of school uniforms and dozens of local athletic league shirts passed through the store, providing a steady flow of income for the aging couple. On a daily basis, Irish widows came by on their walk down Main Street, checking up on sales and occasionally buying underwear, a blouse, a pair of warm socks, or winter boots. Angelica maintained a hot pot of coffee that fueled the gossip sessions of the aging sisterhood.

While it was rare for a black person to shop at the Florence, Tony and Angelica didn't consider themselves racists, especially compared to their relatives, who openly threw around the "N" word at family gatherings whenever America's problems were discussed. Though they had never invited a black person to their house, Angelica did socialize in the parish hall after mass with a Nigerian woman who brought her six children to St. Mark's Church every Sunday. And four years before, Tony had hired a black teen who had been recommended by a local Pop Warner football coach.

For Tony, hiring Chester had simply been good business, as the teams in the football league ordered hundreds of uniforms from the store. And Chester had turned out to be quiet, polite, and hardworking. A few of the customers had been shocked when they first saw the black boy in the store. More often than not, though, his charming smile had conquered the xenophobia so common in suburban settings. The youngster cleaned the floors, ran errands, stacked boxes, and Tony had been giving him more responsibilities until his mother decided to move the family back to Florida. Through his experience with Chester, Tony's mind opened a bit – at least until the following year when a highly controversial school board decision changed the neighborhood forever.

The announcement came down that the locally-based neighborhood elementary school was being transformed into a citywide middle school. Now, each afternoon, instead of seeing cute little white kids getting picked up by school buses, neighbors witnessed a torrent of black and brown pre-teens barreling down Centre Street toward the public bus terminal. Tony had joined hundreds of his neighbors in community meetings to protest the plan. Letters, petitions, phone calls, and emails were sent in a frantic effort, but the final order from the school superintendent could not be halted. The mayor, although sympathetic to the concerns of the white residents, worried about a growing voting block of minority parents, so he kept a safe distance from the controversy.

So now, each school day at exactly 2:45, a mass of students began their exodus up Centre Street toward the station, where they boarded buses for the minority neighborhoods across town: Dorchester, Mattapan, and Roxbury. In a combative mode, the storeowners braced themselves for twenty minutes of loud, raucous chaos. Acutely aware of the school schedule, elderly residents fled the sidewalks, ducking into shops or rushing home. "Imagine, young girls using that language; what's this country coming to," Angelica often complained to the ladies as they chatted over coffee, staring out at the spectacle.

As the tumultuous crowd of hormonally charged kids surged up Centre Street, Tony stood guard just inside his front door. The youth responded to the hateful stares of the shopkeepers by sticking out their tongues, making threatening gestures, laughing, and screaming. In the winter an avalanche of snowballs pelted the storefront windows, as the pack of young people chased, shoved, and wrestled. When one of the kids got pushed against the large picture window in front of the Florence, it seemed the whole store shook. At that point Tony would rush out screeching, brandishing a yardstick in his hand, which caused even louder taunts and howls of ridicule: "Chill, Grandpa! You gonna have a heart attack!" "Stick it up your ass, Gramps."

Tony, for the love of God, never understood the logic of busing these out-of-control kids to this quiet, middle-class white area. On one unforgettable day, he heard an unusual ruckus and looked out the window to see several dozen of them leaping along the row of parked cars on the congested main street—a nightmarish brigade of hooligans, stomping the trunks, roofs, and hoods of one car after another. Of course Tony and his merchant neighbors called the police, but the damage had been done, and the kids had already escaped on the buses.

Just last Halloween, the CVS pharmacy, located a few doors down, had adopted a "two students at a time" policy after about fifty of the kids raided the store en masse and went on a candy spree. On that infamous day, the students boldly raced away with hundreds of dollars worth of chocolate in their backpacks before the store manager even knew they had entered. Immediately after the "Great Halloween Raid," CVS hired an armed security guard to work weekday afternoons.

Eventually Tony had learned to fortify himself for these twenty minutes of chaos each day, but a profound fear and distrust of anyone who was young and dark seethed in his gut.

"Let's take a walk down Centre Street," Tanya said casually, as she and Jada punched out for their one-hour lunch break, a week after their previous visit to the Florence Clothing Store.

Jada gave her a skeptical frown. "Tanya, I'll go with you—but girl, please, no trouble. Let's not scare the folks out here in Whitelandia. Let's just be two professional girls, quiet and polite. You don't plan on returning to that store, do you?"

"Stop worrying about what white people think and let's go," said Tanya as she pulled gently on Jada's braids. After enjoying the "two slices and a coke" special at Mario's, the girls found themselves on the sidewalk with another half hour to kill.

"Let's do some sidewalk shopping," Tanya said, and soon their faces were peering through the spotless display windows of the Florence.

"Tanya, what the hell are we doing here? Didn't we agree we weren't going to start any trouble?" pleaded Jada.

Tanya laughed. "I didn't agree to shit." She sashayed into the store as Jada followed with trepidation. The old woman sat by the cash register munching on a grilled cheese and tomato sandwich. The old man, at his desk, peered over his reading glasses, put the *Boston Herald* on the floor, and stood up.

"Good afternoon," called Tanya without making eye contact, as she strolled towards the back of the store.

The storeowner stared at the young women and followed

from a safe distance.

"Look at all these nice bras," said Tanya, as she worked her hands through a large table display of intimate wear on sale. "I wonder if I can try some on."

She glanced behind her to see the old guy, hands on his skinny hips, standing about twenty feet away in the aisle. His wife had finished her sandwich, and from her perch she also focused her attention on the girls, the only clients in the store.

Tanya continued rifling through the pile of bras. "Jada," she whispered, "stand in front of me for a minute."

"Are you crazy?" Jada answered through clenched teeth.

"Just do it—quick," Tanya ordered.

Jada stepped into the aisle, partially concealing Tanya from the shopkeeper's view. He hobbled to the right like an old rabbit to better position himself. Tanya, watching out of the corner of her eye, made sure that Tony still had a good view of her. Saying to herself, *the hand is quicker than the eye,* she opened her large purse, grabbed a bunch of bras, turned one hundred and eighty degrees, and zipped the bag closed.

"Oh shoot, Jada," she said loudly, "it's late and we need to get back to work."

Adrenaline pumped through Tony's fragile body. Did these girls actually think they could get away with a theft right under his nose? At the same time he was elated that he had caught them. But he had to act fast. He scampered down the aisle towards Angelica and thrust his cell phone into her hand.

"Angie," he said, huffing, "take the phone to the storage room and call the police. Tell them I have a shoplifting incident and to hurry."

"Are you sure?" whispered Angie.

"Just go." Tony grabbed his yardstick and planted himself in front of the exit door.

Tanya, with her oversized black purse slung on her right shoulder, pushed Jada playfully and laughed as she approached the door, but the old man stood firm.

"Excuse us," said Tanya. "We're leaving."

"No, you're not," the shopkeeper fired back.

Jada quivered.

"Dude, you'd better get *out* of that door. I have a job to go to," Tanya said.

"Do you intend to pay for the bras you stuffed into your bag?"

"You're crazy. Now listen, mister, I'm not foolin; you get out of my face and out of my way."

The man raised his yardstick. His wife came running across the room.

"Tony, put the stick down," she pleaded. "The police are on their way."

Tanya glared at the couple and put her hands on her shapely hips. Jada brushed back her long thin braids, took Tanya's hand and started saying the "Hail Mary."

Sergeant Foley, sporting a wide grin, double-parked the cruiser in front of the Florence Clothing Store, lights flashing. For the past two years he had been monitoring the afternoon activities of what he described as "the ghetto kids," and he welcomed this opportunity. He made his way through the gathering crowd of elderly Irish women who were peering in the giant window, but afraid to enter the store.

"Hi, Tony, what have we here?" inquired Foley.

"Hi, Bill," said Tony, his voice shrill. "We have caught a shoplifter here—that one." He pointed a bony finger at Tanya. "She was trying to walk out of here without paying for some bras that she stuffed into her handbag."

Foley, a chain smoker with a massive beer belly, was breathing heavily after the brisk walk from the cruiser. "What is your name, ma'am?" he wheezed.

"My name is Tanya Williams. This is my colleague Jada. We are being detained against our will. You need to arrest this man. He is threatening us." She raised an eyebrow at Tony.

"Please show me an ID."

Tanya opened a side pocket of her bag, produced a wallet, zipped the bag shut, and handed the officer her driver's license.

"So you live in Dorchester, Ms. Williams. What are you doing in this neighborhood?"

"I work here, officer. I work in the Bellevue Nursing Home, taking care of lots of white folks like you."

"Tanya, chill," Jada pleaded as she stood faithfully by, appearing resigned to the reality that her friend was about to be arrested.

"Ms. Williams, my friend Tony here says you have some store merchandise in your handbag. Is that true?"

"It is true. She stuck a handful of bras in her bag," interrupted Tony.

"Ms. Williams, please, do you have this merchandise in your bag?"

"No, absolutely not," Tanya answered.

"But Tony says he saw you do it."

"If Tony has such good eyes, does he know what size bras they are?" asked Tanya, sticking out her impressive chest.

Angelina put her hand to her mouth.

"Ms. Williams, we can clear this up real quick if you'll allow me to examine your bag," said Foley, who couldn't seem to get his eyes off of Tanya's breasts.

"You're not touching this bag if you don't have a search warrant," Tanya fired back, hoping that this line from *Law and Order* would work. "And by the way, I have a sister who's studying to be a lawyer."

Foley shrugged. "All right, Ms. Williams. Then I'm going to have to ask you to come down to the station with me."

"Bullshit, the only place that I'm going is back to work," said Tanya, as she moved to the door.

Now both Tony and Officer Foley blocked the door.

"God help us," prayed Angelica, as Jada continued her "Hail

Marys."

Foley looked behind him out onto the street and saw that the previous crowd of a dozen elderly white women had grown. Now over fifty people were peering in, and the majority of the new onlookers were black and brown teens. "Oh shit," he mumbled, "the McCormack School kids get out early today for the teachers' meetings."

Close to panic and fearing the worst, Foley grabbed his radio and called for backup.

Officer Henry Johnson was driving his cruiser around a rotary about a half-mile from the Florence when he got the call. A black cop with twenty years on the force, Johnson had been asked the week before to help out with the youthful street chaos in the middle-class neighborhood. After three years of deploying white police to monitor the situation every afternoon, someone at headquarters had finally proposed sending a black officer to the area.

Johnson put on his lights and siren and within minutes pulled up behind Foley's cruiser. A tall and athletic middle-aged man, Johnson had been a Division I college football player. Immensely popular with his fellow officers, he was known throughout the city for his prevention efforts with troubled youth in Dorchester. His recent transfer to the white community was a new challenge that he welcomed. He entered the shop and carefully examined the assembled characters.

"What have we got here, Officer?" he asked Foley.

"Hey, Henry," answered Foley. "My good friend Tony here, the proprietor, claims that this Ms. Williams put some bras in her handbag and attempted to leave the store without paying."

"She stuffed a bunch of bras inside her bag—that bag she is holding. I saw her," Tony declared.

Johnson took a deep breath and sized up the situation. Outside, the crowd had grown to over a hundred spectators; most of them were restless young students. Now all eyes, inside and out, turned to Johnson.

"Ms. Williams, what is your first name?"

"Tanya, sir."

"Tanya, do you have any unpaid merchandise from this store in your bag?"

"No sir," answered the suspect.

Foley stepped toward Johnson and pulled him aside. "Listen, Henry, I've known Tony for twenty years. I know what you're thinking, but he's not a racist. Hell, he had a black kid working here for a while. He wouldn't make this shit up. The girl is obviously guilty. If she were innocent, she would have opened up the bag by now."

Johnson nodded and walked back to the door.

"Tanya, can I speak to you for a minute?" he asked.

"Sure." Tanya, with her bag slung over her shoulder, followed Johnson a few yards away.

"You're telling me the truth, right?" asked Johnson.

"Of course; I didn't take anything."

"Well, can we open the bag to prove it to these folks?"

"Why should I?" retorted Tanya. "I've seen dozens of white people shopping here. No one has ever asked them to open their bags. Why should I give in to their racist attitudes?"

"Listen, Tanya, when I go out to any store without my uniform, there is a good chance I get followed too. I understand your anger. I've been there plenty of times. But we have to wrap this up. I want to believe you, but I don't want to take you to the station."

Tanya stood silent for a moment. "Okay, I'll tell you what. I'll give you the bag right now. You take it over to them and let them look inside."

"Good enough." Johnson took the bag and returned to the front area. Tanya joined Jada nearby, who clutched her hand and continued praying. Johnson placed the bag in Tony's arms.

"Here you go, sir. You can look for your merchandise."

Tony set the bag on the table at the register and zipped open the main compartment. The crowd outside pressed against the window, fighting for prime viewing positions. The old man looked into the bag, squinted, and then fished around with his hand. He pulled out a makeup box, a small scarf, and one lonely Trojan that he held up for inspection. Angelica gasped, the crowd outside roared, the two police officers glared at each other.

"Shoot, I didn't even know I had a raincoat tucked away in there. I wonder if it's expired," whispered Tanya to Jada with a giggle.

"I don't see any bras," said Johnson.

Tony frantically began unzipping the small compartments, but found nothing more than Tanya's wallet, a set of keys, and a small perfume sample. The old man broke out in a sweat and looked at Foley.

"I don't understand, Bill. I saw it with my own eyes."

Tanya stepped up, took her bag, and put the items back inside.

"May I go to work now?" she asked tightly.

"Yes, ma'am," said Foley. Tanya and Jada moved toward the door.

"Hold on a minute," said Johnson. "Mr. Dimasi, don't you want to apologize to this innocent woman?"

Tony frowned at the large black officer, then stared at the girls. He froze.

Angelica faced him. "Do it," she said with a calm strength.

"I'm sorry, girls," he spit out.

Tanya gave a curt nod. "Have a great day, y'all." She lifted her chin and strutted up the sidewalk. Several young fans in the dispersing crowd gave her a cheer, but she ignored them. A safe distance away, Jada stopped her.

"Girl, I thought for sure you had those bras in your bag. I thought you were totally busted. What happened to them?"

Tanya shrugged. "Well, yeah, I did grab them, and I did zip up my bag, but as I turned I threw the bras on the floor, under the display bin."

Jada stared at her wide-eyed. "Are you telling me that you set this whole thing up?"

"Sure did."

Now howling, Jada gave her a high five. "Oh my God, Tanya, you are a trip. Well, I guess we can't go back to that store again."

"What, are you kidding me?" Tanya exclaimed. "Next week we're going back there just to make sure Gramps remembers Tanya. And who knows? Maybe I'll actually buy something; maybe I'll buy a bra!"

Mission Hill Neighbors

Paul tilted his head and maneuvered down the familiar steps of the corner store that burrowed into the basement of a six-unit apartment building. He pushed a small jar of Ragu, a box of Barilla spaghetti, and a four-pack of Red Bull across the counter. The Spanish-speaking clerk, with one dead eye and a tilted Red Sox cap, yelled "Happy Thanksgiving, amigo" over the tropical music that blasted from speakers squeezed between packages of diapers on the highest shelf.

"Yeah, you too," responded Paul as he stepped back into the misty night. In spite of his melancholy, he chuckled as he trudged the two blocks to his attic studio apartment. *Ragu and spaghetti*, he thought, *some fucking holiday dinner.* But this option was preferable to his father's gathering in New Jersey.

On the Wednesday night before Thanksgiving almost all of the college students had cleared out of the Mission Hill neighborhood in Boston. Hundreds of apartments in the three-storied buildings stood empty for the traditional break. Precious parking spaces opened up for the remaining residents: elderly Irish, young professionals, struggling artists, and newly arrived immigrants from Latin America, Africa, and the Caribbean.

After climbing the four sets of stairs to his scantily furnished apartment, Paul put the Red Bull in the fridge. The four-pack, along with a gram of cocaine in his desk drawer, provided an assurance— almost a guarantee—that he could elevate out of his chronic funk long enough to produce a ten-page paper due on Monday. He sat on the roughed-up rocking chair that had been left as trash on the sidewalk and pondered his plan for the mini-vacation. As a graduate student in literature, Paul had a routine for getting papers written: Start with a few lines of coke on Friday afternoon, scribble out an outline, brainstorm, and then sip a few beers to fall asleep. Then came a writing frenzy on Saturday, racing through several drafts while sipping Red Bull and snorting at least four generous lines per hour. By late Saturday night he'd print out a solid draft and then chug a six-pack of tall Budweisers to cool his ravaged brain. With the help of the few lines reserved for Sunday afternoon, he'd make minor revisions and proofread.

Planning this unique four-day weekend required some strategizing, however. In addition to the extra time, a wild card appeared in the mix: His dealer had slipped him a generous free sample of crystal meth. While he'd originally planned to experiment after finishing the paper, Paul's curiosity and a craving to jolt his consciousness conquered any logical approach to this novel temptation.

By seven PM on Thanksgiving eve, his fingers trembled with anticipation as he opened the enticing zip-lock bag. Seconds after the first few snorts, he burst into a new uncharted realm, his brain turbo-charged, his mind a locomotive without a track. In a hyper-manic state, he set out to produce a sequel to Dostoevsky's *Crime and Punishment* and wrote furiously for two hours with an ecstatic vision of the Nobel Prize.

The need to share his boundless exuberance led him to call the only colleague he had bonded with at the university. "Come on, Matt," he urged, "let's go dancing."

Within an hour the two graduate students were in a downtown Boston dance club, where Paul alternated between imitating John Travolta and running to the men's room to snort up in a stall. Dancing himself into a sweat-soaked delirium, Paul chugged Coronas and Heinekens. Time catapulted, and he found himself on his knees in a bed, mounting one of his dance partners, a plain looking, girl-next-door type, a thirty-year-old nurse looking for release after her twelve-hour shift in the emergency room. Imagining himself a porn star, Paul drilled her – drilled her through the moans, then the screams. Drilled her till she pulled away and curled up in a ball on top of the sheets. He tried to be affectionate by kissing her cheek.

"Gotta go," he whispered.

"You killed me," she murmured, still shaking. "Please stay a few more minutes."

He stretched out, pulled her into his arms and took a quick look at his watch.

"It'd be great if you stopped by here once in a while," she said, closing her eyes.

After the naked stranger fell asleep, he slipped out of her high-rise apartment, took the final snort, and meandered his way for hours through a maze of streets and alleys back to Mission Hill. Still wired and pacing in his apartment at dawn, he drank a half pint of Jameson before passing out.

The intense high of Wednesday night paved the way for an unprecedented low on Thursday afternoon, as his brain screeched for chemical balance. The excruciating hangover knocked Paul to his knees, from where he promised God, Michael the Archangel, and the Blessed Mother *never again*. He could handle a cocaine weekend, but crystal meth, this satanic beast—no way. He knew that with coke he was flirting right outside of hell's gates, but crystal meth, he now understood, opened the express lane to the very pit of Dante's *Inferno*. Alone in bed, grasping a bottle of Extra-Strength Tylenol for most of Thanksgiving Day, he found something to be thankful for at nine o'clock that night: He had recovered sufficiently to at least sit up, eat some ice cream, and watch football.

In his third semester at Northeastern, Paul focused on survival. He pushed himself out the door on weekday mornings for classes, but when it came time to write papers, he felt stymied; unable to rev up the intellectual engine. With the help of the highly caffeinated Red Bull he wrote several assignments, but then the more potent and reliable cocaine had appeared. At a weekend party he discovered that one of his classmates multi-tasked as an on-campus dealer. Paul bought a gram and snorted several lines to jumpstart a paper on

Oscar Wilde. The sudden insights and clarity of thought astounded him. Ideas leaped from his brain, and words flowed into complex sentences, into coherent paragraphs; then, a few more powdery lines. *So this*, he realized, *was how Freud wrote all those volumes.* Unable to afford a daily dose, he had developed a system. On weekdays he got by on Red Bulls—about four a day—to attend classes and perform his graduate assistant duties. On weekends when he needed to write a major paper, though, he depended on the white blow for mind fuel.

Holed up in the teeming tenement building when not in class, he'd stumble out only to buy minimal groceries and beer. The incessant music and chatter of the Spanish-speaking tenants on the three floors below no longer disturbed him. Dozens of immigrants passed by him on the stairway, but it never occurred to him to say hello or make eye contact. Paul had nothing against them; he had just never considered that they shared the same world. The older Latino adults ignored him, and teenage girls sometimes giggled. Males in their teens and twenties stuck out their chests and stared him down. But Paul remained aloof to their macho posturing. Occasionally, one of the dark-eyed, cinnamon-skinned young women caught his attention for an instant; it seemed that all the pretty ones carried babies.

Back on track after the crystal derailment, by late Saturday night Paul had completed his paper and felt deserving of a reward. With his mind freed from literary analysis, he sensed a creeping, pulsing tension as he popped his first beer. The brief encounter in bed with the nurse had resurrected his sexual appetite. In spite of the constant thrashing of his brain cells, the libido refused to be snuffed out. The stubborn testosterone hung strong and pushed with urgency. Paul had neither the desire nor the capacity to love, but he needed to fuck. A few months before, he'd had a weeklong bed marathon with one of the undergraduate students. But when drama ensued, he'd dropped her instantly. He'd have to seek alternative strategies.

With his athletic build, sparkling blue eyes, curly blond hair, slow deep voice, formidable jaw bone, and charming boyish smile, Paul attracted women with ease. But in his current emotional state he couldn't imagine summoning the energy for the dating process. The nurse had been fun and lively, but he hadn't a clue where to find her. How could he secure a sex partner without going through the mating rituals, the bullshit that got in the way of a good fuck?

A chance browsing of the weekly *Boston Phoenix* that night opened possibilities. While cooling his coked-out cerebral synapses with a forty-ounce malt, he pulled the liberal weekly out of his backpack and found himself reading the adult classified section. Stunned to see dozens of listings for female escorts, one more exotic sounding than the next, his groin stirred. In a semi-drunk and adventurous state, he called a number that promised "International Sex Goddesses". Within an hour he was in a first-floor apartment about a mile away in the Fenway. An older Italian woman with a thick accent welcomed him and brought him into the kitchen. She explained that she had over a dozen immigrant girls working out of the address, with three on duty at any given time. It would be $200 for a half hour or $300 for a full hour.

"A half hour sounds good to me," said Paul as he pulled out a wad of twenties. Led by the madam, he first met a chesty, flat-bottomed Asian girl, who gently rubbed him; next a tall, curvy African, and then a skinny green-eyed Russian. *Wow*, he thought, *where do they find all these babes?*

Keeping with the familiar, he chose Irina, the Russian. While she absolutely forbade him to kiss, she didn't rush him and knew just enough English to make small talk. She even noisily faked an orgasm.

The following Saturday he ached for a repeat performance with Irina. Between his stipend at the college and his father's generous allowance, he estimated he could afford two or three of these adventures a month. After polishing off a six-pack of Coronas he returned to the first-floor apartment, where the madam apologized. Irina had called in sick and she could only offer Lela, a Caribbean girl.

"No problem," said Paul.

Willing, even eager, to sample the darker alternative, he entered Lela's dimly lit room with a brimming curiosity. As his eyes adjusted to the shadows, he saw her standing in front of a bureau. She was young—maybe twenty—petite, gorgeous, barefoot, heavily made-up, and wearing a light, ethereal robe. A long ponytail hung over her right shoulder onto the center of her chest. A beauty mark on her cheek formed God's exclamation point for this marvelous creation. The girl met his gaze and walked towards him. With a wriggle of her shoulders, the robe dropped to the thick wall-to-wall carpet, revealing her full, caramel nakedness. While seemingly weighing no more than a hundred and ten pounds, she possessed graceful, voluptuous curves.

"Take your clothes off, sweetie," she whispered, shutting the door.

Paul obeyed, and she took his hand, leading him to the queen-sized mattress on the floor. As she knelt on the bed, Paul caught a glimpse of her profile in the blue light of a small floor lamp. *I've seen her before*, he thought with a shiver. *Do I know her? Have I seen her on campus? Is she one of my undergraduate students?*

As he lay on his back, she leaned across his body and massaged his shoulders. Again light from the lamp shone on her face; again he was taken aback. He knew this face, but couldn't place it: a countenance of innocence, of pain. He felt an inexplicable desire to enter her world, to know where she came from, how she'd come to this sordid fate. But when he attempted a conversation, she gently spread one hand over his mouth and pressed the index finger of her other hand to her lips. She reached for him, but he pushed her away. He lost his hardness; sex would not satisfy the mysterious need that had manifested. But how could he communicate this? He didn't even know what "this" was.

She remained stoic and disciplined; a professional, she had a job to complete. Against his will, she regained his manhood and mounted him. Helpless, he closed his eyes while she maneuvered him into her. She took off in a sprint, riding him at a furious pace. Transaction completed, she scampered off to the bathroom, leaving him staring at the ceiling, depleted and ashamed, overcome with disgust and self-loathing. He wanted to comprehend the pain hidden under her tough shield but he'd failed. He had wanted to communicate, but she silenced him. Furious with her, with himself, he dressed and rushed out into the December chill, mumbling goodbye, unable to make eye contact. On the way home, her image haunted him. *I've seen her before*, his mind pounded. *I know that beauty mark. But where? In a dream?*

Mission Hill kicked off its holiday season as the mayor of Boston, Santa, and their respective entourages lit the outdoor Christmas tree in front of the Stop & Shop. Students pulled all-nighters before exams and then drank themselves into Jack Daniels heaven. Hard-working immigrants rushed back from Toys "R" Us with minivans full of toys. The young professionals scurried off to endless job-related holiday gatherings. The artists, too poor to shop, darted about, searching for cheap recycled materials to craft gifts.

Surrounded by the holiday rush, Paul had his own mayhem to deal with: Lela. Frantic to know her story, he struggled with his weekly routine. He had entered a new dimension; once the anima is awakened she is relentless. Tornados of uncharted emotions ripped through his being, and her image, her dark eyes, replaced the usual thick fog that clogged his mind. It didn't feel like a sexual or even romantic infatuation. *But what is it? And why?* Somehow this skinny hooker, a stranger who had spoken no more than ten matter-of-fact words during a grotesque business deal, dominated his consciousness.

Paul still drank his Red Bulls and snorted coke on weekends. But when not forcibly engaged in a disciplined activity, his mind drifted to and anchored on Lela. At times he found the obsession profoundly liberating—except for when the anxiety attacks wrenched him out of the chemical-laden web of comfort he had awkwardly stitched together. In those moments of raw panic, he saw no clear path to an even blurrier goal. *This is a prescription for insanity,* he warned himself.

The week before Christmas, Paul's sister Maura called.

Describing a planned holiday reunion at their father's house, she oozed with holiday spirit. His sisters and over twenty cousins, aunts, and uncles were jetting in from various East Coast locations. The clan would be together for the first time since Paul's mother's death—eight years before.

"Pleeeeze come for a few days. Let's just hang out, eat, drink, and have fun—watch *Naked Gun*, play board games, go sledding," Maura begged.

"I wish I could," Paul said, Ebenezer-like, "but I'm buried in work. Sorry."

Paul had three major papers to write over the four-week break. His dealer would be traveling to Los Angeles, so Paul rushed over for a double bag. On the way back he couldn't resist a quick snort in an alleyway. Storming up his stairs with the white fuel tucked in his leather coat pocket, he abruptly stopped on the graffiti-decorated landing between the third floor and the attic. Two young Spanish-speaking women ahead of him were carrying a heavy-duty baby carriage. As one of the women backed up a step to turn the carriage through the small apartment door, she gently collided with Paul as he tried to slip by.

"Excuse me," he mumbled.

"No problem," she answered, shooting him a glance before disappearing into a world of loud voices, Bachata rhythms, and the spicy aromas of Caribbean cuisine.

Paul grabbed the stair railing, his mouth open. Her look, the beauty mark, left him breathless. His heart pounded, his chest heaved, and his knees buckled.

Could that be her? Is Lela living one floor beneath me? Does she know who I am? Has she known all along that I live here? Does she have a boyfriend? Husband? Who are those people she lives with? Was that her baby carriage? No, it's my imagination. Too much coke; I'm losing it.

Up in his apartment Paul paced, but sat down when he realized that Lela could hear his footsteps. He peeked out onto the stairwell, but her door was shut. When he finally had to go out for groceries and beer, he silently darted down the stairs. While terrified at the prospect of confronting Lela, his desire to see her increased exponentially. Huddled in the attic he realized he could never approach her on the stairway, and no way would he knock at her door, asking for milk or sugar. The stomach-churning restlessness, anxiety, and cognitive chaos pushed him to the precipice of a breakdown that beers could not assuage. Finally, on Christmas Eve, he summoned the courage to return to the Fenway.

The madam greeted him and took his two hundred dollars. "Lela's the only one here tonight, but I'm sure she'll make you happy. I'm leaving now; I have a train to catch. When you're done, she will show you out. Merry Christmas."

Paul entered the bedroom. Through the soft blue light he saw her naked under the open robe.

"Take your clothes off," she whispered.

He tried to protest, but his throat locked down. Hypnotized by her steady gaze, he removed his boots and clothes. Her robe dropped to the floor, and she led him to the bed. He lay down, and a gentle wave of perfume overtook him as she snuggled in. Feeling her generous nipples and warm sleek skin slide across his chest, he looked around the room, pleading, praying for a voice.

"Do you live at 38 Hillview Avenue?" he blurted.

She casually shook her head in denial. Her ponytail slid through her hands. When he sat up and peered into her eyes, though, she turned away, facing the wall.

"Didn't I see you in the hallway a few days ago with a baby carriage?" Paul pushed, leaning over to make eye contact.

"Yes," she said, turning back. "My name is Cristina." Terror flashed in her eyes, and she shivered. Sitting up she covered her chest with the sheet.

"I'm Paul," he said, getting up to put his pants on.

"I know."

"How?"

"Your name is on the mailbox."

"The first time I saw you here—did you know I was your neighbor?" Paul asked, returning to sit beside her on the mattress.

"Of course," she said, reaching for an oversized T-shirt. "I remember the day you moved into the apartment. But when you came into the bedroom here the first time, I knew you couldn't place me. You passed me dozens of times on the stairway and never looked; you never really saw me—until last week. And then your expression said it all. But I never imagined you would come back here. When I saw you tonight, I assumed we were going to pretend—to keep it all business like before."

Paul let out a low groan. "No, I couldn't pretend. I just had to come back, to see who you were. I mean are. Cristina, I need to ask you something." He stood up and faced her.

"Okay."

"How did a seemingly innocent young girl get into this situation? I mean . . . it's Christmas Eve."

She looked away, both hands on her ponytail, and abruptly rose to her feet. Then she spun on him, her eyes narrowed.

"Maybe the better question," she hissed, "is how did *you* get yourself into this situation? Why are *you* in a whorehouse on Christmas Eve?"

Paul stepped back against the wall, startled that the girl had the intellectual capacity to formulate such a question. He brooded, searching for an answer, shocked that she had so quickly taken the reins.

"You're the one selling your body," he finally responded, pointing his index finger.

With a quiet determination, Cristina bent over, grabbed one of her high heels, and recklessly fired it at him. Somehow he dodged, his quick reflexes preventing a bloody facial mess, but the shoe's heel caught him on the shoulder.

"What the fuck," he shouted.

Cristina picked up another shoe and cocked her arm, moving closer to Paul, who grabbed a pillow for cover.

"Yeah, what the fuck," she lashed back, forcing him into a corner. "You, a privileged white boy, asking me why I'm selling my body. I need money, okay? I need to survive. Can you relate to that?"

She slashed the shoe at his head, but connected instead with the pillow he used as a shield.

"So what is your reason for being here, white boy? You spend hundreds of dollars to fuck immigrant girls. In your twisted world we're just here to satisfy your needs. Do you like fucking strangers, Paul? Do you like fucking little immigrant girls who act like they are turned on when really they hate your guts?"

Even though she dropped the shoe, Paul continued clutching the pillow to his chest for cover. Cristina picked up her robe and fought to regain her breath. But another wave of rage crashed violently as she circled in front of Paul.

"Your sense of entitlement makes me want to vomit," she screamed as tears streamed down her cheeks. "You think that any of the girls who work here want to be in this hell? Most of us don't have green cards. Where the fuck are we supposed to work? Why are we here, gringo? Have you ever worried about feeding a baby? Have you ever been to my country, the Dominican Republic?"

"No," he murmured, fidgeting out of the corner and backing silently away. Still shocked by the outburst, he met her wide eyes.

"Do you know that we have one of the highest prostitution rates in the world?" Cristina inched forward, tying her robe. "My country is called the Caribbean Disneyland of Sex. Men like you come from all over the world to fuck Dominican girls, and they fuck our guys as well. We're a cheap fuck, we're exotic, we're hot all the time, so say the Internet sites. And we like it. We get all wet just thinking about the gringos who fuck us. A lot of you perverts like young children. You bring them to the hotels — girls and boys nine, ten, eleven years old."

Paul held up his palms. "Whoa, that's sick. I'm not into —"

"So sex tourism is a major part of our economy," Cristina

barreled on with her hands on her hips. "And you know who owns the travel agencies and the resorts, beaches, and hotels where all these sex tourists go? Americans—they are the ones who cash in. You all—Americans and Europeans—have turned our island into a sex playground, and most of the country is dirt poor. So you and me, amigo, we're playing out the same sick scene right here in Boston. Immigrant girls serving the nasty pleasures of fuckers like you. And you, you son of a bitch, have the balls to ask me why I'm here!"

She fell silent, gasping, opening and then slamming the top drawer of the bureau. Speechless, Paul sat down with his hand over his mouth and stayed silent for several minutes. He felt diminished with each insult, stripped of his manhood; his existence shredded. But somehow, through his dark tangled complexes, he found a voice.

"You can make all the damn excuses you want," he slammed back, standing up and buckling his belt. "You can blame the white man for everything wrong in your life and in your country, but what about you taking responsibility for yourself—for your own actions?" He took a step toward her. "You made the choice to be a slut. You made the choice to open your legs for any asshole with a wallet full of cash. You're not eleven years old; you are an adult. When are you going to take control of your life?"

"Shut up, shut up," Cristina screeched as she pounded the top of a bureau. "I hate you, I hate you! I hate all you bastards who think we are toys. You are a fucking loser. Most guys who come here are old. You are young. Where is your girlfriend?"

He halted and maintained a few feet of distance. "Yeah, congratulations. You've discovered that I'm fucked up. You want to know more? I'm a fucking cokehead. A cocaine addict, okay? That's my excuse. Does that make me more like you now? Does that make me more ghetto? That I'm all fucked up? Does that somehow make us equal? This conversation is worthless. I'm getting the fuck out of here."

Paul hurriedly pulled on his sweater and fumbled with his boots. Cristina sat in a fetal position in the bedroom doorway, shaking and whimpering.

"Merry fucking Christmas," he sputtered as he grabbed his jacket, stepped over her, and advanced down the hallway. He struggled with the lock on the exit door.

"Please . . . don't go yet," Cristina said with gentle authority, her voice hoarse. Her command abruptly shifted the ambiance and Paul paused, subdued.

"How long have you been on coke?" she whispered.

"About a year and a half," he said. He turned and stepped back over her into the bedroom.

"Hmmm, about the time I got started in this shithole."

Paul returned to the mattress, where he sat with his untied Timberlands pressed to the floor. Cristina remained crouched in the doorway. For more than five minutes neither spoke. Paul stared at his feet. Cristina rested her head on her knees. Swirling Arctic winds whistled through the cracks of the old brick apartment building. Finally Cristina walked to the window and pushed back the curtain.

"Oh my God, it's snowing."

Paul joined her to view the first flakes of a forecasted blizzard; all of Boston was braced for a true New England nor'easter.

"I'm sorry I hit you," she said, gently rubbing his shoulder.

"Yeah, don't worry. You really went off, but I was a jerk. I apologize."

Cristina took his hand and led him back to the bed. She helped take his boots off and they sat side by side, propped up by the half dozen pillows against the wall.

"So really, I don't get it. You're a young, good-looking guy. I'm sure you can get all kinds of ass for free. Why are you here?" she asked, pulling her hair back.

Paul shrugged. "I don't know. I saw the ad in the *Boston Phoenix* and what can I say? It's cowardly, and I hate myself for it. But the last time I came here, something happened. I felt crazy because I knew I had seen you before, but I couldn't for the life of me place you. I just wanted to talk, try to understand. Maybe I figured that if

I knew why you were here, it would somehow help me understand why I was. Ever since that first night I've been wanting to talk to you. Then, oh my God," Paul continued, throwing his hands in the air. "I see you on the stairwell. I'm like, Holy shit, she lives in my building. That freaked me the fuck out. So here I am. I was determined to talk to you, and I figured it was easier here than on the stairway."

"And what about the coke?" she asked, setting her hand on his knee.

"Why am I on coke? That's a good question." Paul rubbed the back of his neck and then his head. "No one ever asked me that. Shit, the only other person who even knows I'm on coke is my dealer, and obviously he doesn't give a fuck. Let's see, I got hooked when I started graduate school here in Boston. After I got my bachelors, I guess I fell into a depression of sorts. I never thought about it much. Funny, I studied psychology and couldn't even diagnose myself."

"You studied psyche? I've always wanted to study that."

Paul raised an eyebrow. "You did? Yeah, it's interesting."

"So why were you depressed?"

Paul sighed, turning to lie back on the mattress. "Lotta reasons, I guess. After college my girlfriend moved back to Texas, so that fell apart. I went back to my family's house in New Jersey, where I tried looking for a job, but there wasn't shit for an undergraduate psychology major. So I just moped around by myself, realizing how empty my old house felt. My mother had died of cancer when I was sixteen. My father was always working or out with his girlfriend, and my sisters had moved on. I'd just fritter away my days wondering where all the warmth and love I had grown up with went. So for about a year, I just hung around, working a couple of days a week with a friend who owned a small construction company."

"You didn't find a new girlfriend?" asked Cristina, lying on her side, her head propped up on her elbow.

"No. A few girls came by my house once in a while, but nothing serious. They were sweet, but I had no desire for a relationship. I had nothing to give. So about a year and a half ago, my father takes me out to dinner and says, like, 'What's up? What are you doing with your life?' I didn't have a fucking clue. But we decided that I'd go to graduate school and he offered to pay, so it was off to Boston."

"You came by yourself?"

"Yeah. I thought I'd be excited about studying again, but I just couldn't find the energy to do the work. By chance, I tried a few lines of coke—then bang. The blow becomes my best friend."

"And you didn't find a girlfriend in Boston?" asked Cristina, leaning in closer.

Paul winced. "I'm a fucking mess. I've had a couple of flings, but I can't handle the drama, never mind the commitment. So one night I'm buzzed on coke and beer and I end up here with the Russian girl. Then the next time I see you. Like I said, it was driving me crazy, because I knew I had seen you before."

Paul excused himself, went to the bathroom, threw some water on his face, and returned, standing over the mattress. He looked down at Cristina, wondering how she could have pushed a baby out of her petite frame. *I should go,* he thought.

"So Paul, you still want to know how I got into my mess here?" Cristina patted the mattress next to her.

He sat on the rug and leaned against the mattress. "Of course. If you want to tell me."

"I'll tell you." She smiled tightly. "You know anything about my country, the Dominican Republic?"

"Not much," he said. "I know it's somewhere in the Caribbean. My college friends did spring break there. You know, the beach, the bars; they were drunk the whole time."

Cristina rested against the wall and wrapped her arms around her knees. "Figures; that's how most foreigners view my country—as a place to play. Anyway, I came here to Boston from the DR when I was six. I vaguely remember saying goodbye to some guy they said was my father, even though he never lived with us. I haven't seen or heard from him since. I was thrown into first grade with all English-speaking kids—sink or swim. I guess I swam, since my mother was there every night to tutor me. She worked full-time cleaning houses, getting documents together, trying to get us legal. We lived in Roxbury in public housing with two of my aunts, an uncle, and a bunch of cousins. Meanwhile, my mother got together with a really nice Dominican guy, Enrique. He was hard-working, responsible, and he tried to be a father, tried to make us a family. But he was undocumented and he had a minor car accident—no license, no registration. The Boston Police turned him over to la Migra, U.S. immigration. They detained him for three months, then boom— deported. My mother went into a deep depression, barely kept her job. But she's a survivor, and she gutted it out for me."

"Wow, so your mother lives with you now?" asked Paul.

"No, she's in the DR. I really miss her, but we talk all the time. Anyway, when I was fifteen I fell in love with this dude – Bomba. We were together for about a year and he was my prince, but when I found out he had lots of princesses, I freaked out. I cried for weeks until my cousin introduced me to Leonardo, who was twenty-seven. I didn't really like him, but being with him eased the pain of losing Bomba. Within a couple of months I was pregnant. Leo told me he loved me, would get me papers and would provide for me. He never gave me shit – not a cent. He kept coming by the apartment after my baby was born, looking for ass. I didn't say no to his booty calls until about a year and a half ago, when I started this job. After a day's work on the bed here, you can imagine I told him to fuck off. He's since gone off and gotten another girl pregnant—a Guatemalan girl."

"Did he know about your job here?"

"Are you kidding me? He'd flip out, beat the shit out of me. I'm sure he would tell my whole family and the rest of the world. No, I've managed to keep this a secret, Dios mio. I've only shared my story with one Brazilian girl, Rosa, who I used to clean office buildings with. We still get together once in a while for beers. Other than Rosa, you are the only person in the world who knows. Irina, and all the other girls here, none of them know Cristina or where I live; they only know me as Lela. I even have a separate phone for work."

"Does your kid's father still come by the apartment?" Paul asked as he crawled across the mattress and sat at her side.

"Yeah, he comes by to see my cousins once in a while, but I don't look at him. I don't talk to him. He pretends to play with my baby. She wants nothing to do with him."

Paul paused, wondering if he had possibly passed the ex-boyfriend on the stairway. Spontaneously, he slipped his hand over her palm and intertwined his fingers with hers. She smiled and continued.

"So about two years ago my aunt gets evicted, cause her son was dealing. The twelve of us scrambled for a place to live. My mother was a mess and went back to the DR, where she married Enrique. I am happy for them, but I was left here with my daughter. She was a fussy baby — slept all day and screamed all night. I thought about asking my cousin Sonia – who's married to a Puerto Rican fire fighter – if I could stay with her. But I didn't want to bother them; they already had four kids in their house. I had no place to live, no money, still no documents, no job, no food stamps, and a baby that cried all night. We ended up in a shelter for a couple of months. Dios mio, I hated it. I finally got a job cleaning office buildings downtown at night for ten dollars an hour. The company sends a van out to the ghetto to pick us up and deliver us to the sites. Sometimes we'd have to wait more than an hour in the cold for the assholes to come get us. I had a Dominican girlfriend who offered to rent me a room in her apartment in Dorchester, so I went for it. I also paid her to baby-sit Milagros while I worked. I had a lot of debts. I had borrowed from everyone I knew."

"Your baby's name is Milagros? That means miracle, right?"

Cristina's face softened. "Yes, she is my life; she's two and a half now. I'm sure you've heard her cry. You'll meet her. Shit, she's your neighbor. You've seen her, right?"

"Yeah, I think so. What happened then?"

"So there was a Dominicana, Lisa, living in the apartment with us. One night we're drinking beers after work, and she tells me she's making fifty dollars an hour giving massages. I'm like, 'What?' Here I was killing myself for ten dollars an hour. Lisa said she could get me in, so I went with her. They gave me some training in massage for about a half hour and told me I was ready. We were in this so-called medical building over on Commonwealth Ave. I was given my own room with a massage table, and right away I got my first client, an older white guy. I should have figured it out when he immediately got naked and lay on the table. I started massaging his neck, shoulders, and back like I had been trained, and the next thing I know, he's turned over with a big disgusting hard-on."

"Holy shit," Paul gasped, tightening his grip on her hand.

"He says, 'Fifty for a handjob?' I freaked out and ran to find Lisa. She took me to an office and told me straight up what the deal was. I would get paid by the tips from these guys. She pleaded with me to give it a try—just for one day—and then I could make up my mind if I wanted to stay. I was furious at her; even more furious at myself that I could be so stupid. Later I found out that she got a thousand-dollar bonus for recruiting me. Anyway, I had to make a quick decision: run out of the building or go back to the client and make my first fifty bucks. I made over four hundred dollars in six hours. Of course, Lisa knew what she was doing when she asked me to try it. At the end of the day, you realize you have already been corrupted. You've crossed the line. You're already a whore, so why bother stopping."

"Jesus," Paul whispered.

Cristina's head fell into her hands and she breathed deeply. She then turned toward Paul.

"Hey, you hungry?"

"Yeah, you got something?"

"Let me go see."

She came back with Cheez-its. "Oh wait," she said, skipping out to the hallway mantel.

"A Christmas gift from one of my regulars," she laughed, holding up a box of chocolates. She placed the goods between them on the bed, along with a quart of Poland Springs. Paul leaned back against the pillows in the corner. She positioned herself in front of him, wriggled between his long legs, and put her head back against his chest.

"So I started coming to the massage parlor four days a week for six-hour shifts," she continued, munching on Cheez-its as Paul started on the chocolates.

"Some days were busy; others slow. You don't want to know the details, but let me just say that once you do a sexual act with a man for money, you will pretty much do anything if he puts enough cash in your hand."

"No, I don't want to know the details," Paul responded as he gritted his teeth. Emerging images of Cristina on top of old, fat naked men disturbed him greatly.

"So I learned how to be a full-fledged whore pretty quick. For some reason the massage parlor shut down after a few months, but I was already in the network. Melia, the madam here, recruited me right away, and I've been here ever since. When I first started working here, a year and a half ago, I was desperate. I had debts, bills, I had rent, I had my daughter. With all the money I made, I paid off my debts. I bought a little Honda, baby clothes, all sorts of toys, got me a nice wardrobe, and bought my mother a car down in the DR."

"Wow, that's generous."

"I love my mom. I told her I'm earning this money in a beauty salon."

Paul thought about asking her why she stayed in the job, but his intuition flashed a stop sign.

"Ayee," Cristina continued, leaning back on Paul as he played with her thick hair. "Every week I tell myself that this is it. I should look for another job. I just need to let go. But I can't explain it. This job gets a hold on you. I hate it; you can't imagine how much I hate it. But it's like an addiction; I keep coming back. Each morning I wake up and I'm horrified that I have to face another day here and I don't know how I will possibly force myself to go. Then I have coffee and start to think what else can I do that day. I think about the hundreds of dollars I could make. And then I think, I'm already a whore, I will always be a whore, I can't escape my past. So I get dressed up and come here. My life sucks. I have to get out soon, though, or I'll go crazy. I can't live this way, always lying to people. I can't let down my guard for one minute; I have to be an actress. My family would die if they found out. I have to think about my daughter; she sleeps with me every night. Imagine the ghosts and demons I'm bringing home. And God forbid, what happens if the police bust this place? They'd take my b-baby away for sure."

Paul felt Cristina trembling. Leaning over and looking down, he caught a tear from her cheek with his baby finger and instinctively wiped it against his lips before tightening his embrace and gently kissing her head.

"Aye, Dios mio, Paul," said Cristina, turning around and kneeling in front of him. "You have to watch it with coke. That shit can really fuck you up."

"Yeah, I have to deal with it."

"You look healthy and strong. Quit now, before it hooks you. They got programs to help. I've had friends who beat it."

Outside the winds continued to howl and the snow accumulated rapidly.

"You're reading this?" asked Paul, picking up *The House of Spirits* from a pile of books stacked beside the mattress.

"Yeah, I love to read. My mom's a reader. She's a teacher back home. She always surrounded me with books. They've been my escape."

"This is a good escape," said Paul, leafing through the novel.

"Oh shit, it's eleven o'clock." Cristina jumped up. "We should go."

"You want to walk?"

"Yeah, we have to. I doubt the buses are running in this crazy snow."

A city is never so beautiful as it is a few hours into a blizzard.

Only those bold enough to venture out feel the full impact of nature's cleansing, when billions of heavenly sparkles offer a fresh start to those who tune in to the magical benediction. Arm in arm, Paul and Cristina plodded rhythmically up Huntington Avenue, creating a new path in the virgin sidewalk. The silent streets were interrupted only by the craziest of immigrant taxi drivers who still hadn't grasped the concept of snow. Covered in white, without hats or gloves, the couple warmed up in a pub.

"You frozen?" asked Paul, stamping his boots near the bar's fireplace.

"No, I love snow," Cristina said, shaking her hair. "During my first winter here I loved it, and I've loved it ever since. I don't get how people complain about it. It energizes me."

They shared a grilled cheese, French fries, and a bottle of red wine.

"My God, I feel like I'm on a date," said Cristina. "Do you know when was the last time I had a real date? Like when I was sixteen—three years ago."

"I don't remember the last date I had," said Paul.

The wine gave them the courage to start out on the last leg of their journey. The dancing white bands continued to circle them as they reached the base of Mission Hill. Before starting up the daunting slippery slope, they paused, hearing the sounds of a choir and organ. Across the street the faithful were celebrating a midnight mass at the Mission Church, Boston's most beautiful and elaborate cathedral.

"Let's go in for a minute," Cristina urged.

"Okay. You Catholic?"

"Kind of. You?"

"Ya, sort of. I'm Irish, right?"

Inside the church, in a timeless trance, they crowded in behind the last row of pews. As the mass progressed to the Gospel reading, she took his hand. She pulled him through the crowd over to the far left wall, next to one of the confessional booths, which had a small cloth window. Paul watched as she took the madam's apartment key, pushed it through the cloth, and he heard its subtle clang on the floor. Then she knelt down beside the booth, closed her eyes, and bowed her head. After several minutes, she rejoined Paul, who stood mesmerized, drawn to the life-size image of the Blessed Mother at the center of the main altar, adorned by a bright sea of red and white roses, carnations, and poinsettias. The glowing white marble figure showered a beneficent radiance. His senses competed to absorb the multidimensional aesthetics: the aroma of the fir wreaths and two massive Christmas trees on each side of the nativity scene, hundreds of flickering candles, the bright stained-glass panels illuminated by exterior flood lights, the pervasive and mysterious incense, the gentle aroma of Cristina's perfume, her head pressing into his chest, the melodic message of hope from the organ and choir.

The embracing presence of Mary, the queen of Catholic goddesses, penetrated his consciousness, and he smiled, allowing her luminous and perpetual comfort to return. For the first time since his mother's death he felt her intense warmth, her laugh, her saintly spirit. With her compassionate eyes serving as mirrors into her soul, his mother had welcomed her kids, relatives, and friends to the kitchen table where she served tea, Irish bread, and wisdom. Torrents of emotions, buried for years like his mother, rushed through his body. A riptide of joyous tears delivered a relief he had not believed possible.

How had he allowed her death to extinguish that flame of magic, the comet of love that had grounded him within the grace of his soul? He looked down at Cristina and felt her hand squeeze his. Candlelight danced across her honey-gold face. He felt a shining certainty that a new path had opened. He squeezed back.

How can I hold on to this moment? Paul repeated to himself. *I have to come back here — often. This is my sanctuary.* The thought of sitting alone, in the quiet of this magnificent structure, brought him great comfort.

"I need to get home," Cristina whispered.

Outside the blizzard continued, as whirlpool patterns created sculptured drifts on the porches of the triple-deckers, where Christmas lights glowed under the thick, angelic dusting.

At the Hillside Avenue apartment building they stomped their feet, then ascended the stairs to the third-floor landing. Inside Cristina's apartment music pulsated.

"My cousins will be partying all night, but I'm going to cuddle up with my daughter and sleep. My baby will be waking up early to open her presents."

She leaned in and stretched her thin, strong arms around him. He gently brushed the snow from her hair and shoulders.

"Thanks for the date," she murmured with a wide smile.

"Thank you," he answered, leaning over and kissing her forehead. He began trudging up the steps, but stopped and turned as she unlocked her door.

"Cristina."

"Yeah," she said, gazing up the staircase.

"I'm gonna leave to visit my family early tomorrow morning. I should be able to get on a Greyhound. But when I come back, in a week or so, maybe you could come up for a coffee?"

"I'd love to."

"I'm gonna need support to b-beat th-this," said Paul, his voice cracking, his eyes watering up. "I've got one hell of a fight in front of me."

"Yeah, me too. Dios mio, we both have a tough road ahead. I've got a lot of soul-searching to do. But hey, we're both right here, okay?" She gave him a thumbs up.

"Yeah, and we've got the church down the hill." He turned to look out a small hallway window.

"It's beautiful," said Cristina with sparkling eyes. "I can't believe I never went in there before."

Paul nodded gently. "Okay, Cristina. Merry Christmas."

"Merry Christmas, Paul."

A Good Hair Day

I met Jada in a kung-fu class over at Northeastern. Rick, the young aspiring master, had studied in China and charged only a few bucks per class. We used an aerobics studio at the gym that was packed with eager students and two older professors. A no pain-no gain torturer, Rick led a robust ninety-minute workout that had us swearing, sweating, and struggling for oxygen. After a few weeks the timid disappeared, and only Jada and I remained as his regulars.

"This is okay," said Rick. "I'm not looking to make money. I just want to get some teaching experience under my belt. I'd rather work with a small group of serious students."

During our three sessions each week we went through a stretching and conditioning routine before a series of kicking, blocking, punching, and throw-down drills. As the classes progressed, Jada and I developed a camaraderie and mutual respect, nurtured by the intensity of the classes. Jada is an attractive girl, but her frequent mention of a fiancé helped prevent any of my fantasies from going over the top. Thin and petite, she had extravagant long, thin braids that swirled around her head and occasionally whacked me in the face during our combat practice. One Friday as we left the gym soaked in sweat, I mentioned to Jada that I needed a haircut. She glanced up at the mess on my head, grimaced, and then laughed.

"You know, Matt," she said, "my mom and I cut hair on weekends. Our specialty is black women's hair, but we can take a white boy."

"You're on," I said, grinning back. "Where's the shop?"

"It's in our kitchen." She handed me the address.

Jada's Jamaican family resided in a working-class neighborhood in Mattapan, only a few blocks away from a Red Line extension trolley. When I arrived on time for my noon appointment the kitchen was packed with black, Caribbean, and African women of all ages, sizes, and shapes. They spilled out into the attached living room, chattering as they got their hair dried, cut, colored, shampooed, curled, straightened, braided, and God knows what else. None of them gave me a second look. Both Jada and her mother, Deidre, dashed between rooms armed with all sorts of metal and plastic tools of the trade. Deidre ignored me until I took a seat at the kitchen table.

"Moms," announced Jada, "this is my friend Matt. He wants a cut."

Deidre gave me a quick glance and continued working conditioner into a client's scalp. Feeling more than a bit uncomfortable, I picked up a *People* magazine and started reading about Angelina, Brad, and their African kids.

"Jada," Deidre barked suddenly, "wash his hair."

Jada led me over to the double kitchen sink, pushed my head under the faucet, and began rubbing in some shampoo that smelled like Hawaiian Punch. Her older sister, busy at the stove, drew close to drain a pot of rice by pouring the boiling water into the adjacent sink, inches from my face. A cloud of steam engulfed my head. I jumped back and shot Jada a "What the hell is going on?" look.

"Relax Matt," she said. "Part of the deal here is that we feed these women lunch. Taking care of black women's hair is a day-long event."

Clearly not a black woman, I hoped to spend no more than a half hour. Being white and male, I assumed that with my shampoo completed, either Jada or Deidre would immediately tend to my needs so I could carry on with my day. Shit, I had a long to-do list to get through. After several minutes of punishing my scalp, Jada used the sink spray hose to rinse and handed me an already-used damp towel.

"So Jada, I'll be getting cut soon, right?" I asked with a tone of authority, shaking my head dry.

"Matt, chill," she responded, pushing me out to the living room. "Can't you see that we have eight women who were here before you? We'll let you know when, okay? For now, you can watch TV or get a magazine."

Within minutes after I got comfortable in an armchair, three women entered the room and sat on the large sofa facing the television. Patrice, a forty-something Nigerian woman, stood at about five-foot-eight, had shiny dark skin, and moved with a natural smooth rhythm. Though slightly overweight, she still had a well-defined figure that I noticed under her long blue and white summer dress. She wore a lush afro and big silver earrings that glowed like her eyes. Listening to some side conversations between Jada and Deidre, I deduced that Patrice would be getting braids. Even though Patrice ignored me, I felt a warm maternal aura behind her serene smile and made the assumption that she was a great mother.

After Patrice settled on the couch, in strolled Shaniqua, who seemed about twenty-five. She had a pretty face, was a bit lighter-skinned than Patrice, and I guessed that she got to the gym once in a while, judging by the muscle tone of her arms, shoulders, and legs. She wore skimpy jean shorts over black stockings, a thick gold necklace, and a tight white sleeveless top that allowed for several inches of bare abdomen. My immediate thought on her stomach was: *Maybe less French fries and more sit-ups before going public.* Her medium-length straight hair had a blond streak. She projected an attitude, but it wasn't nasty; more of an attractive and provocative sassiness. *A fun party girl,* I thought, studying her worn flip-flops—*first and last to the bar and the dance floor.* Shaniqua nuzzled close to Patrice on the sofa as if they were sisters and started clicking through the TV stations.

I struggled to control my stare when Marie entered. A tall Haitian girl, she resembled a model—thin, with tantalizing curves and a flawless, angelic face. She wore conservative black dress pants and a red blouse that buttoned to the top and matched a red ribbon in her long, straight hair. Her stylish high heels also matched, as did the belt around her micro-waist. She projected a dignity and sense of confidence rare for a girl in her early twenties. *How can such a beautiful woman seem so pure?* I wondered. My sensitive nose picked up an aroma from Marie that was as enchanting as her physical presence — had to be a Parisian perfume.

After the shared embraces, kisses, and gentle laughter with Patrice and Shaniqua, Marie gracefully sat at one end of the sofa. Shaniqua continued clicking until she came across one of those entertainment celebrity gossip shows — a story about the Chelsea Clinton wedding.

"Whoa, Bill Clinton's getting a little older, but he's still looking good," said Patrice, leaning over to turn up the TV volume.

"Girl, if I was Monica Lewinski," said Shaniqua, lounging back on the couch, "I would have done the same thing. I'd of gone right down on him, gobble him up, and enjoy every second."

"I'd do Bill in a heartbeat," said Patrice, throwing one of her legs over the side of the sofa, dangling her bare foot. In general, white men don't do it for me, but Bill, mmm mmm . . . he's got a black soul."

Marie sat up, her back arched, and met Patrice's eyes. "What he did was disgusting. He's married."

Shaniqua put her hand on Marie's leg, lowered her chin, and raised her brows. "Yeah, he was married all right. Obviously Hillary wasn't taking care of business under the presidential sheets. Bill is gorgeous, charming, and could have any babe he wanted. Shit, what man in a position of power wouldn't take a bite of the apple, or should I say cherry?"

"No way," said Marie, standing up to face the other two. "A marriage vow is sacred, and marriage is for life."

"Girl, what do you know about marriage vows?" asked Patrice, throwing her head back and letting out a deep laugh.

"As a matter of fact, I'm getting married next month," responded Marie with her hands on her hips.

Shaniqua gently took Marie's arm and guided her back to sit on the couch.

"Damn, people still be getting married?" she said, struggling to get a flame out of her cigarette lighter. "I haven't been to a wedding in five years. All my married friends already been broke up."

"Hey, hold on," said Patrice. "I'm still married. So Marie, are you marrying a Haitian?"

"Yes, we've been together for three years," said Marie, folding her hands.

"And honey," asked Patrice, leaning towards the young Haitian, "how old is he?"

"My age, twenty-three."

At that moment, Jada jetted into the room, looking frantically for a particular pair of scissors.

"Hey Matt," she said, tapping me on the head as she rushed by. "You getting a crash course on the intimate lives of black ladies?"

For the first time all three clients glanced at me, but just for a second. I felt the blood rushing to my face and wished Jada would leave and let me go back to my invisible man status. This was getting interesting!

Patrice carried on, content to ignore me: "Well girl, I hate to be the one to tell you. All men play, but Haitians, mmm mmm. Lots of my home girls went out with Haitians, and guess what? *All* of them lied and all of them were already married. They lie, lie, lie."

Marie rested her head on her palms, listening intently.

"Haitian fuckers are no worse than any others," chimed in Shaniqua. "They all the same. They all try to cheat; it's just that some got the game to do it and others don't. A good-looking brother, particularly one with a hefty salary—shit, he's a magnet for chicks, whether he's married or not. And I have yet to meet a dude who will say no when opportunity knocks. You want a man without game? Okay, maybe you can keep him in the house. But who wants a man with no game?" She blew out a stream of smoke as she finally got her cigarette going.

"My fiancé got game," said Jada proudly, passing by again to pick up the scissors she found on the carpeted floor.

"Huh," said Patrice. "What Shaniqua's saying is right, and the sooner we realize it, the better off we'll be. In Africa they don't call it cheating; it's polygamy. I've been married for twenty years, and I know my husband messes around. Right now he's got a young twenty-five-year-old bitch he's been running with. My God, he's twice her age. He hasn't told me directly about her, but he doesn't hide it either. I even know her family."

"You allow this?" asked Marie, opening her arms as if crucified.

"Honestly, girl, what do I care?" answered Patrice, taking Marie's hands between hers. "He's a good husband. He pays the bills. He's a responsible father. And even though he's in his fifties, he's still got strong needs; always did, always will. Me, at this point in my life I only need some love a couple of times a month and I'm good. So this young girl takes the pressure off me. Now he's not pokin' around at night when I'm trying to sleep."

"Well, you shouldn't be allowing that," said Marie, her sweet voice rising. "Plus, he must be spending money on her."

Patrice gave a shrug. "He's a hardworking man," she said, as convincing as a defense lawyer. "He works eighty hours a week. He keeps his obligations to me, pays the mortgage."

"But your children; how old are your children? How do you explain this to them?" asked Marie, her eyes wide.

"My kids are nine, eleven, and seventeen. They know their daddy doesn't come home every night, but they know if they need him, he's there. His children have always been his priority — that's the sign of a real man."

"Well, to each his own," said Marie sitting back, arms folded. "But I've found me a good man. We're going to have a strong spiritual marriage in the Catholic Church and bring up our children in a loving, stable home."

Patrice's smile turned to a low, throaty laugh. "Good luck,

sweetie," she said, though not unkindly. "I'll give your guy about three years before he starts sniffin' around for pussy — new pussy. You can have the sweetest, hottest, most delicious pussy in the world, but they always want *different* pussy. You're a pretty girl, but at some point he's gonna start chasing ass, even if he still loves you."

While Marie pouted, Shaniqua stood up, turned off the TV, lit another cigarette, and began to pace in front of the couch like a professor.

"I don't think this marriage concept works anymore. In fact, I don't think I'll ever live with a man again. I used to be insanely jealous of my man. I've had two long-term relationships, and both times I thought I was in love. We lived together, had great times, but I caught both of them cheatin' — fuckers. I exploded and left. When they cried and pleaded, like an idiot I went back; but then it was déjà-vu all over again. I had to go through a hell of a lot of pain to get where I am, but I feel strong now without a man. I've got a good job; I got my apartment, my Toyota Celica. So who needs a man?"

"C'mon now, girl, you know that's not the whole story," said Patrice with a mock frown.

"Sure, I have a couple of friends; hey, I got my needs." Shaniqua chuckled, running her hand over her crotch. "But I call *them* when I want a visit. I have a nice professional forty-something guy who is very generous — and oh, by the way, he's married. This dude knows how to romance: nice dinner in a chic restaurant, expensive wine, conversating, and slow, expert lovemaking. Nothing like a smooth, sweet-talking, experienced man in bed. But I also got me a nineteen-year-old boy toy — this kid round my way — who's a lot of fun. My own little sex slave. He'll do anything I tell him — anything. But these two dudes come to me on my terms. I'm done making commitments to men, because they just plain can't fuckin' keep them."

"You're seeing two men at the same time?" asked Marie, looking up. "Do they know about each other?"

Shaniqua continued her pacing. "I made it clear that I'm not looking for a monogamous relationship, so I have nothing to hide.

You want a shocker? I have some lesbian friends, and every once in a while I sleep with one. Now, I don't think I'm lesbian, cause I truly like dick — *real* dick. But let me tell you, sometimes it's nice to go to bed with someone you can actually talk to, who can open up about themselves. I'm still looking for a man who can hold a decent conversation about his feelings for more then thirty seconds."

"Shaniqua, you got it going, girl," said Patrice, stretching out her legs. "Maybe if I was young I'd be more like you. But I'm tired at night after a full day of work, cooking for the kids, helping the younger ones with homework. I plunk myself down in front of the TV. If my kids are healthy, I'm happy and I sleep good whether my husband's home or not. My husband takes care of me and knows exactly what gets me off in bed, so I have no need to look around. He's a warm guy; always has a hug, a joke to tell. He'll sit with me in the kitchen, have a cup of coffee. I know he loves me and he's nice to have around, but I don't need him every day. There's a guy at my job who wants to mess with me and I thought about it, but I just don't have the energy. But who knows? If he keeps talking and I get curious, maybe we'll get freaky some afternoon in a hotel room." She laughed, gyrating her hips.

"Well, some day I may find Mr. Right and try to trust again," said Shaniqua, kneeling in front of the couch. "And in the next few years, I'd like to have a kid. If I find a good, honest brother who is stable, has a profession and wants to share a child with me — no problem. But I don't need him living with me. Who knows, maybe I'm just afraid of getting hurt, but I honestly don't mind living by myself. If I'm living with him, I'm always going to be thinking about where he is, what's he doing, who he's with . . . I don't need that aggravation. Been there, done that."

"Ladies, ladies, you're forgetting something," said Marie, pulling Shaniqua back onto the couch. "Marriage is about commitment and promises. Of course in our lives we will have urges to look around, but it's our responsibility to control those feelings: for the good of our partner, for the good of our children, for the good of our extended families, and for the good of ourselves. God gave us free will, and we can choose to be faithful. And if we create a lifelong spiritual union, the doors are open wide to God's grace."

"Girl," responded Shaniqua, playfully slapping Marie's leg. "I would love it to be that way, but it ain't. If men held up their end of the bargain, I would too. Home girl, I don't know if you are naïve, blind, or just in love. Your vision is every girl's dream, but one day we wake up and find that it's a fucking myth. Men are dogs, plain and simple. I don't like it, but that's the way it is. We have to protect ourselves, keep our independence: financially and emotionally."

"I don't think men are dogs," said Patrice. "They're just different than us. It's in their nature to roam. Why can't we just accept that? Sweetie, that is a beautiful vision you have," she said, reaching across Shaniqua to take Marie's hand. "I wish you the best and I respect your point of view. But as someone who's more experienced, I have found that sometimes you have to settle for what's real, not the ideal. If you shoot for the ideal and expect nothing less, you are setting yourself up for a very frustrating and bitter life."

But sitting straight, Marie held her ground: "I have faith in the institution of marriage and I have faith in God. I don't think we should just give up and expect that men will always break the sacred vow of marriage."

"Marie, let me ask you something. You grew up in Haiti, right?" asked Shaniqua.

"Yeah," responded Marie with some trepidation.

"Did your father stay loyal to your mother?"

"Well, that was the old days," said Marie.

Shaniqua poked a finger at Marie. "So did he?"

"He had another woman, over in the next town," Marie admitted, her eyes aimed at the floor.

"Uh huh," said Shaniqua, rising to her feet, "what we're talking about. You need to wake up, girl. I would love for you to have a successful marriage, but don't be blind."

Marie sniffed, then replied in a haughty tone. "If you expect a man to act like a dog, then he will. It's a woman's role to lead him to a more spiritual level. Yes, he may make mistakes, but you have to forgive and believe that with God's grace, he will overcome temptations and the marriage will lead to a deeper bond."

"Girl, don't talk to me about forgiveness," said Shaniqua, sucking her lip. "You don't know how many times I forgave. I'm done. Forgiveness just encourages them."

Patrice shook her head. "You do need to forgive them," she said. "But even more, you need to understand them."

I never did get to hear the end of the girl talk session, as Deidre hollered out from the kitchen, "Matt, come in here!"

While Deidre passive-aggressively cut my hair, a tall middle-aged black man with a beret arrived at the apartment. He was ignored by everyone except Jada, who greeted him with a generous hug and kiss.

"That's my father," whispered Jada, passing by as she went back to attending her clients.

The man moved quietly in the kitchen and took a plate of rice and meat.

As he retreated to a bedroom down the hall, Deidre yelled out, "Where you been?"

"Work."

"All night?"

"Yeah, double shift," he answered, shutting the door.

"Double shift my ass," yelled Deidre as the kitchen erupted in laughter.

After Deidre finished and I paid my fee, Jada followed me into the hallway.

"Matt, you look good. Not bad for ten bucks," she said, sliding her long fingers through my hair. C'mon outside with me while I have a smoke."

Barefoot on the sidewalk, wearing black gym shorts and a white T-shirt, she leaned against her father's Escalade and lit up a half joint.

"So, you gonna become a regular here, Matt?" She smiled.

"Yeah, I could. Just I didn't expect to spend two hours," I said, leaning back beside her.

"But you weren't bored, were you?" she asked, skillfully blowing the smoke to the side.

"No, it was actually quite a fascinating conversation."

"Yeah, I heard bits and pieces as I jumped around. Just normal black women beauty shop talk."

"It's normal that they talk about all that personal stuff in front of me?"

Jada looked perplexed. "Why would they change their conversation just because you're waiting in the room? That's just the way they are."

"Yeah, I guess. Just that it seems complicated," I said, scratching some loose hair clippings off my neck.

"No, Matt, it's actually quite simple," said Jada. "We just want what everyone else wants—love and respect." She took a deep hit before flicking off the burning tip and sliding the remaining butt into her shirt pocket.

"Okay, Matt, I got to get back up," she said before I could reply. "We'll be going strong into the night; still a lot of hair to get through. I'll see you Monday at class."

She got on her tiptoes, kissed my check, and hurried back to the apartment. I headed off to the trolley, trying to picture Marie at Sunday mass with her family - in five years, in ten years, in fifteen years. . . .

Love Campaign

When the pain is unbearable, fantasies come to my rescue: He'll surprise me with a creative romantic scheme—just like in *Pretty Woman*. Then we'll have a massive wedding and a houseful of kids. Or the fiancée is killed in a plane crash and I rush to his apartment, patiently nurturing him through the mourning period. Then, a month later he tells me that I, in fact, have always been the true love of his life. Then there are darker imaginings related to the violent elimination of her.

The mind-play provides short-term relief, but like the *Titanic* hitting the iceberg, I invariably crash into the frigid realization that Kevin has moved on, sending me down, down, down into a numbing ocean of despair. It's ironic that his voice, stubbornly implanted in the core of my consciousness, still comforts me: "It's best to welcome pain, accept it, own it.... Pain is life's method of teaching.... With pain comes an important lesson.... Stay with the pain and it will lead to a new awareness, a new strength." I can see now that even at our peak, he wanted to prepare me for the inevitable. He's down in Washington, working on the transition team. Probably end up working in the White House. I saw him on TV, up on stage at one of the inaugural balls. He looked damn good in that tuxedo.

I'll be okay; at least that's what my therapist, my mom, and Jada tell me. I'm back in school now, and I know the healing process is in motion because I'm starting to talk to a couple of guys; just talking, but I find solace in their company.

In May of 2008 I finished final exams and I ended the short-term strained relationship with Carl. Desperate to find a summer job in Boston, I sent out over twenty resumes. While I waited with optimism, I volunteered one night a week downtown in the Obama for President campaign office, mostly entering data and making phone calls. On a Thursday night, at about nine o'clock, a dozen of us were debating which bar we'd invade at Quincy Market when the office manager asked for our attention and introduced Kevin, the New England campaign field coordinator. What was he, I wondered, a light-skinned brother, a Latino? Was he Italian, or from the Caribbean, maybe the Middle East? In his gorgeous brown suit, he grabbed everyone's attention. This election, he explained, was Obama's for the taking. We had an historic opportunity, and in the next six months the future of the country — the future of the world — would be decided. But, he argued, we needed a massive mobilization to get our man, our movement, into the White House.

As he spoke I felt his confidence, his arresting charm, and his boundless energy. He made a passionate pitch for volunteers to go up to New Hampshire for the weekend to door-knock and reach undecided voters. With Massachusetts already a solid blue state, we had to take our energy across the border to conquer our battleground-state neighbor.

About half of us signed up that night for the trip. Being my usual inquisitive and aggressive self, I lingered on the way out, drawn to his smile, his magnetic masculinity. Handsome and well-groomed, with the shortest of hair, he stood about six feet tall. He had a graceful, wiry, muscular body with a well-pronounced butt – a butt that could mesmerize you on an escalator, a butt that got you fantasizing about having little baby boys with that same butt. As we sipped Diet Cokes, he told me that he practiced law with a Boston-based firm and had taken a leave of absence to campaign. His penetrating warmth and intensity – call it his aura – made me shiver.

Kevin had met Obama eight years before, in Chicago, where he had served as an intern in his State Senate office. Then, last winter, the candidate had called Kevin at five o'clock in the morning and asked him to take this role in New England. Of course I found his story and his personal connection to Obama captivating, so I was shocked when he inquired about my life. His clear, light brown eyes twinkled with interest, grounded in the moment. After giving him the basic details, my curiosity overpowered me. "So what are you? I mean culturally," I asked.

He laughed. "Like Obama, I'm quite a mix," he said. "My mom is black and my dad is Puerto Rican. One of my grandmothers says there's even a little Irish in there somewhere."

"Wow," I blurted without shame. "What a great genetic experiment."

I left the headquarters that night with a new excitement, not knowing if its source was Kevin, the campaign spirit he embodied, or some mysterious combination.

Two days later, at six-thirty AM, I'm on a packed bus, headed to Concord, New Hampshire. I had to love how all those white folks were supporting our guy – and they were pumped. By eight-thirty the bus arrived at Obama headquarters, and a bug-eyed middle-aged campaign worker, Sully, announced that the volunteer coordinator for the day had fallen ill—something about his heart. He asked if anyone wanted to assist him in coordinating the day's activities. Standing next to Sully, holding my fourth cup of coffee, I said, "I'm down, Sully, Let's do it." Apparently I did a kick-ass job, because later that afternoon Kevin offered me the volunteer coordinator position.

"But I've never worked on a campaign before."

"Tanya, it's clear that you have the essentials for the job; you have a take-charge attitude, great people skills, and high energy," said Kevin. "Besides, in a turbo-charged campaign, we don't have time to do job searches. We need a replacement—not tomorrow, but now."

"So I would work right through to November?"

"Yes, if you can take the fall semester off. Fulltime, twenty-four-seven. There are no days off. Maybe a few hours here and there to attend to personal issues, but basically, we don't stop. The pay is okay—six hundred a week, plus three meal vouchers each day and always a decent hotel room. But you won't have a life other than the campaign."

How could I say no to this man-god? My own petty life could be put on hold; hell, we had a mission to carry out. We shook hands, and I called to thrill my mother, a big Obama fan. I then had twenty-four hours to wrap things up in Boston and return to Concord.

For the first few weeks we mostly visited college campuses on a frantic schedule. I'd arrive at a campus alone and spend a few days putting up posters, and checking in with dozens of political, environmental, and ethnic student organization leaders, liberal and black faculty, and black religious groups. Then I'd reserve a large room and buy a mountain of pizza and Coke. We'd usually attract a crowd of a couple hundred. Then Kevin would magically swoop in to make the volunteer pitch. I watched the young crowds, catching alight as Kevin fired them up about the movement sweeping the country. He not only rallied the Obamanic crowd into a frantic "Yes We Can" chant, but he convinced us all that we were making history. I don't know how, but when Kevin spoke he made every single person feel that they were needed, that they formed an essential link in this chain of change. I stood behind him amazed at how he engaged the audience and commanded their awareness. Hundreds of eyes beamed as he persuaded them to join a higher cause, a calling, and he generated an undeniable electric spirit. He spoke about the transformative quality of the campaign, how people were relating in new ways, riding this wave of emotion and optimism. The American people had been alienated from their government, but they were now taking it back, getting on board the train of hope, the locomotive of progress. After Kevin's rousing twenty-minute speech I'd follow up with a more down-to-earth explanation of volunteer opportunities.

My political IQ rose exponentially as I began to truly grasp the enormity of our undertaking. Leading the richest, most powerful country in the world, Bush had really fucked things up: ignoring global warming, spawning a new generation of terrorists in Iraq and throughout the Arab world with his wars, sending the economy into a freefall with skyrocketing unemployment, propping up the banks that had caused the collapse, further enriching the wealthiest few. The lines had been drawn between the two parties, and the political knowledge I gained fueled my passion. When you believe in a righteous cause, when you understand the opposing forces, when you believe you are on the side of justice, you somehow find unlimited energy to engage in combat.

This exuberance soon spilled into my personal life. After being at his side for about a month, I found it increasingly difficult to mask my mounting sentiments toward Kevin. As a nineteen-year-old healthy female, I ached for attention, and just a glance from him or hearing his voice got my juices flowing. Damn, other than a brief interlude with Carl, I hadn't truly pressed flesh with a man for months.

My sexual experience had been limited to a few adventures in high school which were first scary, then fun. I still hadn't experienced that head-over-heels heart-throbbing tension.

But ever since my boobs seemingly popped out overnight at the age of twelve, I had been well-schooled on the sexual urges of the male species. For years my God-fearing, Jamaican mother had repeated on a seemingly daily basis: "Girl, you stay away from boys, and don't you ever walk into this house and tell me you're pregnant unless you're married and finished with college." In my early teens I had picked up the basics of sex education from girlfriend-chatter and quickly mastered the art of dodging incessant and often perverted aggression. I'd sprinted out of the basement of the Victory Baptist Church after Deacon Williams fondled my butt. I creatively avoided Mr. Henry, my seventh grade history teacher, who created a myriad of opportunities to brush against me. I refused to make eye contact with the scar-faced ex-con at the local convenience store, who regularly offered me free porn magazines. I ignored the sixty-something owner of the neighborhood pizza shop when he told me that I resembled his ex-girlfriend.

In the eighth grade, I had sucker-punched Reggie, a family friend, for spontaneously stroking my breasts. And I repelled, ran from, cold-shouldered, and sent to hell the dozens — if not hundreds — of men of every conceivable age, ethnicity, and race who pulled over on the city streets to offer me a ride. I even spit a mess of Hershey and saliva onto a long-haired freak who stroked himself in his car while asking for directions.

But in spite of this overexposure to the dark side of male cravings, I held onto a faith in and a vision of true romance. I had reached the limits of the recreational sex with the sweet-smelling pretty boys, the hard-muscled tough guys. My young soul cried out for passion, and I prayed fervently for the love of my life to appear.

Yeah, Kevin was more than ten years older than me, but there was no ring on his finger and never a mention of a girlfriend. I had plenty of gay friends, and Kevin just didn't project that vibe. From what I could see, he slept alone every night. God knows he had opportunities; I saw women swooning over him every day. But when a powerful hottie is declining to dip into the wide-open benefits inherent in the fast-paced heat of a political campaign, something had to be up.

In my ever-increasing fantasies, I invented the notion that he was waiting for me to make the first move, so I set my plan in motion. Every couple of days I'd steal a half hour, get downtown, and buy a new top, a new push-up bra. If I knew on a particular day I'd be spending time with him, I'd show more of my cleavage, more of my flat abs. I strategized to get his eyes focused on the rose tattooed on the small of my back. I bought a few light summer dresses that set off my long, toned legs. I desperately wanted him to see me as a woman, not just another campaign worker.

After a grueling day in Portland Maine, we arrived at the Marriot Hotel at about 10:30 and checked into adjacent rooms. In the hallway he kissed me on the cheek and said good night. I knew that after a sixteen-hour day, Kevin loved to read mystery novels before falling asleep. As I showered and slid the soap bar over my body, I pictured him on the other side of the wall, stretched out in his boxers. After drying my hair, I called and asked if he could open a bottle of wine for me. He strode into the room shirtless, barefoot, wearing only his suit pants, with his reading glasses on top of his head. His sculptured six-pack matched beautifully with the V that started at his waist and expanded up to his chest and shoulders. He seemed a bit startled upon seeing me in my skimpy pajamas. As he opened the wine I purposely leaned over to get a glass, providing him a full view of my free-swinging boobs. The tension in his face proved that my sensual trap had a good chance.

"Kevin, have a glass of wine with me," I said. "You need to unwind."

"No thanks, Tanya, I'm beat. Another night."

Just like that he turned around and left. I gulped down a quick glass to ease the shock. It was the first time in my life that I had been turned down by a male. Too exhausted to stay awake, I collapsed into oblivion, thank God.

No time to brood or pout. We had a seven AM meeting, so I put a muzzle on my desires. Shit, we had a president to get elected, and I couldn't let my selfish personal needs complicate matters. Besides, Kevin traveled to Rhode Island for four days while I stayed in New Hampshire. About a week later, though, we joined up in New Haven, Connecticut. We wrapped up by nine o'clock that night, in time to watch the Celtics and Lakers in the NBA Finals. Kevin invited me to watch the game, and I said sure, that my room would be fine. A few minutes after the tip-off, he arrived with a twelve-pack of Heinekens and a large bowl of popcorn. We sat on my massive king-size bed, propped up against a mountain of pillows. Luckily we shared a hate for Kobe and a deep love for the Celtics. Our green team got hammered in the second quarter, and were down by twenty-eight.

At halftime I casually announced my need for a shower, and Kevin just nodded, staying focused on Magic Johnson's analysis. I came out twenty minutes later with a large white hotel towel wrapped around me.

"Hey, the Celtics are making a run," he said, staring at the tube, seemingly unaware that I stood before him half-naked. Indeed, the Celtics had cut the Lakers lead down to fifteen; maybe it would be a game after all.

Still in my towel, I sat on the edge of the bed and used the hair dryer during the commercials. As the fourth quarter started, the play-off intensity reached a frantic level, pulling us into the nationwide drama. We roared together when Paul Pierce ripped the ball from Kobe and went in for a dunk, tying the game. We matched Kevin Garnet's defensive intensity by slugging down the beers at a reckless pace. We high-fived and hugged when Ray Allen hit his third consecutive three-pointer. In the last two minutes the Celtics cemented the lead, cruising to a victory, and we hooted and bounced on the bed, creating mayhem. At the final buzzer, as the Celtics celebrated the greatest come-from-behind win in NBA playoff history, Kevin playfully slammed a pillow into my face. I responded by spontaneously forcing a wild kiss, which he readily accepted. As I knelt on the bed with my hands digging into his shoulders, my towel dropped and I didn't care. He opened his eyes wide, then pulled away, rolled over, and sat on the edge of the bed.

"Tanya, we need to talk."

"Okay," I said sheepishly, pulling on an oversized Celtics shirt. I turned off the TV, reached to get each of us a beer, and sat beside him.

"Tanya, I find you a very attractive woman," he said, his voice cracking, "and believe me, spending the last month with you has been great. But there are a couple of realities we need to deal with."

"Like what," I fired back, facing him boldly.

"First of all, I'm ten years older than you, and —"

"That's nothing," I interrupted.

"Okay, fine, but there is another issue." He paused and gulped. "I'm engaged. My fiancée, Caroline, is in graduate school right now — in Paris. She'll finish in June, but she's coming back to visit during the holidays."

"That doesn't surprise me. How long have you been together?" I asked, standing up.

"We've been together for over ten years, on and off. We've both been involved with other people at times, but our friendship is constant. She is my best friend and my soul mate. We plan to get married and have kids together after she's finished her studies."

"Isn't it difficult being away from each other?" I pushed, sucking down beer and trying to ignore his use of the term "soul mate".

He shrugged sadly. "Yeah. Over the past decade we've often been living in separate cities and we've had all sorts of arrangements. Right now we have agreed to keep things open. In other words, we have a 'Don't ask, don't tell' policy. We are secure with each other and our long-term commitment."

I fought off an extreme desire to know her race. I pictured her white, then black, but then thought, *sista in Paris....not.*

Keeping the conversation going, I asked: "Don't you get jealous?"

Kevin nodded. "Jealousy is always there, but we're tight. Let's face it, we're young and have needs. We are both extremely busy, but honestly, if she has a friend over there, I can deal with it. I don't want to know the details, but if something happens three thousand miles away, it's okay. In the future, when we share the same house and have kids, I'm sure we'll stay monogamous so nothing gets complicated. But we have agreed to continue discussing this issue as we move through life. Whatever we've done for the past ten years has worked. We're still in love; we're still together."

"So does this mean you are free to have something with me?" The fifth Heineken had made me bolder.

"Tanya, I like you a lot, I have a strong attraction to you. But I've been fighting my urges. I'm afraid of hurting you and myself. I'm thinking it may be better to stay friends and co-workers. I worry that we could get into something too deep, since we spend so much time together. Then boom, it will end after the election. I think it's dangerous. We have to work together almost every day, right?"

"Kevin," I said, in my most persuasive, seductive voice, as I opened yet another beer. "I've had casual sexual relationships. I can handle them. Hey, we're here together."

"Tanya, you are sweet. But let's think about it. We're both half dead now and we've got a long day tomorrow." He gave me a kiss on the cheek, said good night, and left.

Dejected, but with hope still alive, I popped another beer and watched the post-game interviews. Ten minutes later he was back.

"Tanya, do you have any body lotion?"

"Sure, in the bathroom."

With the lotion in his hand he sat on the edge of the bed, turned off the TV, and told me to lie on my stomach. Slowly, he initiated me into the sensual pleasures of foot massage. I lay there, feeling his strong fingers work each toe, sliding between them, applying pressure to all the points on the bottom of my feet. Completely sedated, I couldn't remember ever feeling so relaxed, so comfortable. Never again would I under estimate the power of a man's hands. After forty minutes of bliss, he leaned over, kissed my cheek, and said, "Now you'll sleep in peace."

I barely heard the door shut as he slid out. I awoke the next morning wondering if I'd dreamt about the massage, but the body lotion on the night table provided confirmation.

For the next five days, Kevin raced through Vermont and Rhode Island while I stayed in Connecticut organizing students. On the weekend, we both arrived back in New Hampshire at the Marriot. That night he knocked on my door about midnight and asked if I wanted another foot massage. He spent about a half hour on my feet and moved up to work on my calves. He skipped over the thighs and buttocks and spent another half hour on my back, neck, head and shoulders. Again I felt deeply relaxed and this time flooded by a roaring carnal river. But he kissed me on the cheek and returned to his room.

The next night I took charge. I knocked on his door, he warmly welcomed me in, and we shared a bottle of wine. Sitting on his bed, we watched CNN's coverage of the campaign and then, without warning,

I made my move. A woman possessed with rampant hormones, I closed my eyes and kissed him recklessly, losing myself in a fury of desire. He seemed hesitant and remained passive, letting me attack. I tore my clothes off as I slobbered him with kisses. Weeks of pent-up tension exploded. Blind with heat, I reached violently for his belt, but he shocked me by pulling away.

"Hey," he whispered, laughing gently, "slow down; there's no rush. I'm losing you. You're going off on your own like a train wreck. Let's stay together."

Slightly embarrassed but unrepentant, I giggled and fell back on the bed, catching my breath. Tamed for the moment from my savage needs, I took his cues, and we spent our first full night together in our underwear. We hugged, kissed, whispered, dozed off, and woke up, drifting in and out of various euphoric states. He squeezed me, sometimes with all his force, sometimes with a masculine delicacy. He played with my hair, scratched my back, and found my ticklish areas. He examined my hands, sucked my fingers like a baby, and played with my earrings. He kissed me throughout the night on my neck. Sometimes we'd doze off, staring into each other's eyes, and when I'd awake, his eyes would still be there. We barely had two hours of sleep in total, but I got up at six AM, rested, refreshed, and hungry to get out on the campaign trail. Over coffee I felt an attachment, a closeness that I had never felt for anyone. My heart glowed and smiled; a fire radiated throughout my body.

We spent the next three nights together, and he conquered me - oh my god did he conquer me - at his pace. Now it didn't matter anymore how and when we made love. I remember those nights under the covers in our underwear as the most intense, dreamlike episodes of my life. I don't even remember which night it finally happened, but when it did, it was just a natural extension of all the emotion and closeness we had built.

From then on, whenever we landed in the same city, we spent the night together. Although I started to travel more with Kevin, I would only see him in brief glimpses during the day. He commanded from the top levels, while I scurried around somewhere in the middle, handing orders down to the volunteer masses. At night when we unwound together, we had endless stories to share about the wild cast of characters we worked with. Every campaign attracts not only the good, the bad and the ugly, but also the neurotic and psychos, who provided unending gossip.

In our private moments, Kevin most often moved in slow motion, bringing time to a standstill, teaching me to cherish each second. Once in a blue, if pressed for time, we'd have a fast and ferocious ten minutes. On wild nights we'd turn up the music full blast and dance around the room in our underwear, daring each other to take another shot of whiskey. Then in bed, we'd drink the Johnny Walker off each other's bodies.

With Kevin, I learned the secret ecstasies of love; that it came down to being open, to letting go of all inhibitions, to being able to surrender myself fearlessly. He usually treated me like a goddess, but when necessary, he'd also let me be an animal.

Every morning I woke up with boundless energy. I hungered for the opportunities to talk campaign strategy with Kevin, and I learned a lifetime of politics during those six months. We had the *Boston Globe*, the *New York Times*, *USA Today*, *Newsweek*, and *Time* spread all over our bed. We tracked the poll numbers in the battleground states. We constantly clicked between CNN, Fox News, and MSNBC, analyzing the latest polls and rating the commentators. Kevin had access to internal campaign documents, and he took the time to review them with me and explain the strategy debates within the campaign hierarchy. I learned the details of Obama's economic recovery proposal, his plan to address global warming, and his ideas to revolutionize the health care system. I understood the tremendous power of the presidency and how new, creative thinking could address our nation's most pressing problems.

No doubt, Obama rocked; how the hell else could a black man have risen so quickly, shattering centuries of barriers? He shocked even the most liberal optimists with his lead in the polls against an authentic American war hero, a white man with thirty years in the Senate. I developed the capacity to imagine the changes that could be made within a White House led by a compassionate and shrewd genius. As September approached, I sent a letter to my college, explaining my decision to take a semester off. No way in hell I'd leave the excitement of the campaign; no way in hell I'd leave Kevin.

"The energy is there. We just have to ignite it and ride it," Kevin told anyone who would listen. In late September, campaign central sent Kevin to Pennsylvania — the mother of all the battleground states. They wanted him to tighten up the field structure and organize a series of rallies. I traveled with the campaign on a whirlwind tour of seven cities in three days. With hundreds of details and tasks for each rally, we had an excruciating workload, but the energy transformed us all. I finally understood how Obama kept his frantic schedule day after day, week after week. The energy from the crowds exploded and pulsated through all of us. And the African-Americans in the crowds moved me most deeply. I never tired of seeing the tears of wonder, beaming faces, and pure joy emanating from my brothers and sisters who truly believed they were witnessing and living a miracle: the possibility of an African-American president in their lifetime.

In bed, after each exciting and exhausting day, as I merged my body with Kevin's, I explored, processed, screamed, and sobbed my way through this unique experience. In the heat of the night, I felt the campaign's power, I felt Kevin's power, and I felt my own. I never received a resolution to the question that constantly pounded my brain: What is the source of this magic? Kevin or the campaign?

Kevin talked about the famous Kissinger quote that "Power is the ultimate aphrodisiac." At times I wondered if I'd be so wild about Kevin if he'd just been a regular campaign volunteer, instead of one of the top dogs. Some nights as I showered before getting into bed with him, I thought about the magnetic quality of his voice, how he could move a crowd with his clear, persuasive language, how he carried the power of the campaign in his walk. And the thought that each day dozens of women hit on him pumped me with desire to claim, conquer, capture, and possess him. Yes, he's mine, I reminded myself with glee—at least for now, until that uppity bitch in Europe comes back. I understood that much of Kevin's power came from the sharpness of his mind. The memory of him propped up in bed, plowing through a pile of newspapers with his reading glasses on, is probably the sexiest image I hold. I knew that no matter what happened between Kevin and me, any man of mine in the future would need to have an active intellect to keep me interested and involved.

While women in the campaign swirled around Kevin, I also got hit on regularly. As a young woman who takes care of herself, I had plenty of admirers. With my new masculinity radar, I sensed who were the boys—those who talked shit in their ego-driven attempts to find a few moments of pleasure—and who were the men, those who truly communicated with a woman, and knew how to be open, give, receive, and respect. After engaging for just a few moments with a male, I had the awareness to know whether he had mastered the delicate art of intimacy, if he knew how to make a woman feel like a goddess, if he truly listened, if he knew how to love her mind and heart. Once a woman experiences real love, she'll never settle for less.

Two weeks to go, and Obama looked good. We spent most of our time now in Ohio and Pennsylvania, the two largest battleground states. With New England solid, the campaign wanted Kevin's skills fully utilized. Thank God, polls showed that with the economy collapsing, the majority of voters trusted Obama over McCain. A bursting sense of optimism permeated the campaign, but we were reminded again and again to not let up, to fight for every possible vote. Kevin told me in private that Obama's top advisors were assembling a transition team to be in place the day after the election.

On the Tuesday night exactly two weeks before the final election, Kevin and I got to the Sheraton in Columbus, Ohio at about ten-thirty. We sat on the bed and sipped wine, swimming in newspapers, while Anderson Cooper interviewed a panel of election experts on CNN. Without warning, Kevin cleared the bed and turned the TV off.

"Tanya, my dear, we should talk," he said, setting his glasses on the night table.

"Okay," I said, refilling the wine glasses.

"In two weeks, this is over. We're going to win, and I've been asked to go to Washington on the transition team. I'm going to be part of the vetting machine, making sure all the cabinet nominees are clean. There's talk of keeping me in the White House as an aide."

"Wow, sweetie, congratulations!" I said with a bursting pride, leaning over to kiss him. He kissed me back, but not with the usual gusto.

"Baby, there's another thing I need to tell you. Caroline is coming in for the holidays. She plans to arrive in Washington for Thanksgiving, and then she'll be staying with me until she goes back to Europe in January. I have to find an apartment somewhere in D.C."

Just the mention of her name sent a pain to my chest that shot up into my head, causing me to gulp the full cup of wine; I did my best to stay composed.

"Well, we knew it would have to end, right?" I said, hoping he didn't notice the quiver in my voice. "We can still enjoy the last two weeks."

"That's what I'm worried about; if it ends too abruptly. I wonder, Tanya, if we should ease out over these two weeks. Maybe try to go back as friends."

"Kevin, you don't have to worry. I'm strong. We knew this was coming. I know it's going to hurt, but until it happens, I just don't know how much."

"What are you going to do? School doesn't start up again until January."

"I've got family in Barbados and Jamaica. I'll probably chill for a few weeks down there. Then I'll just get one of those holiday retail jobs in Boston and get ready for school."

"Tanya, I know we've both been completely honest from day one, but I still feel like shit. I feel like I'm abandoning you, and it's not a good feeling. If I let myself, I could so fall in love with you; actually, I think I already have. I think I love you, Tanya." He paused and met my eyes. "I know I love you."

"And I know I'm in love with you," I confessed, fighting the tears. At that very moment I jumped my boy and put an end to the talk of a gradual breakup; he offered no resistance. Breaking-up sex is painful, but still the best.

During the last two weeks of the campaign we worked eighteen-hour days, and by the time we took showers, processed our daily adventures, and had our romp in bed, we only had two to three hours of sleep.

In Philadelphia on election night, two thousand of us packed into the largest function hall in the downtown Hilton. Kevin warmed up the crowd but refrained from declaring victory prematurely. CNN streamed in on a massive screen, and a raucous cheer erupted each time new numbers came in. Now the only drama left was which state would put us over the top. Just before ten o'clock, Wolf Blitzer, the dean of political analysis, said the magic words: "CNN is now projecting that Barack Obama will be the next president of the United States."

A massive wave of euphoria swept the crowd, with hugs, kisses, shrieks, and literal jumping for joy. The moment carried me as we watched the president-elect, his breathtaking wife, and his adorable kids come out on the stage in Chicago. A tsunami of tears flooded the room as Obama stepped up to acknowledge his victory and gracefully pay respects to McCain.

Kevin and I went upstairs just before one o'clock that morning. I took a quick shower and waited naked for him under the covers, anticipating our own private celebration. It seemed like forever, but when he finally he came out of the bathroom he wore boxers and a T-shirt. I reached for a nightgown, put it on, and got back into bed. Kevin had a plane to catch at seven the next morning, so he'd need to leave the hotel at five. After a minute in his arms, the tears starting rolling, and then came the sobs and full body tremors. He buried his head in my hair. I felt his body shaking. His tears strangely provided me a soothing consolation. Instinctively I gave him my breast to suckle, feeling empowered to provide a primal sedative to my boy as we lay wrapped up in silence like a couple of lost puppies.

At four-thirty his cell phone alarm sounded. He quickly showered and packed his two suitcases. He shook me gently as I lay on my side. I continued to breathe deeply with my eyes closed. He leaned into me, kissed my forehead, and whispered, "I love you" — and then I heard the door shut; the most painful click of my life. Minutes later I got up and made some coffee. Never had I felt such a staggering sense of emptiness. I threw on some clothes, trudged down to the lobby, bought an assortment of newspapers, and returned to the room. Reading about the election miracle, seeing Obama's victorious smile, and watching a glorious sunrise over Philadelphia brought some relief. Some.

I went back to Boston and spent two weeks with my best friend Jada and my mom. I told them both about Kevin, giving Jada more of the juicy details. I realized that talking through my experience with the two women who love me unconditionally kicked off the healing process. The Caribbean also proved to be therapeutic. I floated alone for hours in the ocean off the coast of Barbados and Jamaica, praying for God's comfort, pleading with him to bring me back to life. As always, he heard me.

Now back in school, I'm trying to stay occupied. The two political science courses I'm taking are fascinating, and in our study groups I'm talking to a couple of friends.

Am I bitter? Don't think so. Don't want to be. Kevin never lied; in fact he is the most open, honest human being I have ever met. He concealed nothing, and he treated me like a queen. I seduced him. I demanded the intimacy, fully aware of the risks and inevitable outcome. I still love him today, and I will love him forever.

The suffering has eased in recent weeks, and I'm starting to eat again. I lost over ten pounds, and edged dangerously close to being as skinny as Tyra's sickly top models. I still get the dagger flashes, the psychic stabs, and I expect they'll continue, but ease out. After all, the six-month relationship rocked my core. It stripped down, twisted, and wrung out all my rookie adolescent understandings of love. The amorous alchemy I shared with Kevin crystallized my entire being. I entered emotional and spiritual chambers I never knew existed.

So, you might ask, if given the choice, would I do it again?

In a heartbeat.

Merengue!

Having attended Catholic schools through twelfth grade, I planned, of course, to continue at a Catholic college. Not quite Notre Dame material, I breathed a deep sigh of relief after getting into Boston College, a prestigious Jesuit-led institution. By my sophomore year in the early 1990's, I had settled into campus life and chosen political science as my major. I lived on the third floor of O'Leary dorm, surrounded by a familiar pack that had coalesced during freshman year. We also had some new faces, including two dark-skinned Spanish speakers who roomed together. When they smiled at me, I'd smile back with mild curiosity. It never entered my mind that I would walk into their room, sit down on a bed, and start talking like I did with the white kids. Plus, passing by their door I only heard incoherent babble and some loud strange music. The two Latinos just didn't mesh into our comfortable tight white tribe.

But my diversity-deprived consciousness expanded later that autumn when I saw Julio and Octavio at a campus-wide event. As an aspiring political activist I attended a meeting that featured MIT Professor Noam Chomsky, lecturing on U.S. foreign policy. At the packed meeting I discovered that my dorm-mates not only spoke fluent English, but also won the respect of Chomsky with their brilliant analysis of U.S. intervention in Latin America.

After the meeting I walked back to the dorm with the two cousins and immediately we forged a strong camaraderie. They explained that in the mid 1960s, over 40,000 Marines had invaded and occupied their country, the Dominican Republic. In the 1970s their fathers had participated in a popular movement that opposed and challenged the U.S.-backed regime. After spending three years in jail, the two activists and their young families escaped to Manhattan to begin a new life. Growing up in Washington Heights, Julio and Octavio enrolled in a Catholic high school and excelled academically, becoming the two top scholars. Through some influential Catholic politicians, they obtained green cards, and in their senior year a prominent New York philanthropist had arranged full scholarships to BC.

During that semester we got close. The cousins were two to three years older than me, so I had the role of the younger brother. In addition to politics, we bonded through sports, partying, and girls. Access to my social network provided a renaissance of sorts for the Dominicanos as they crossed ethnic divides and met a steady stream of white Irish-Catholic coeds, several of whom eagerly welcomed their first multicultural sex adventure; their first bout of "tropical fever." Plus, the gringas could conveniently practice Spanish 101 under the sheets. So my two amigos stayed quite active during the week. On weekends, however, they clicked instantly into monogamous mode when their drop-dead-gorgeous Dominican girlfriends, Bianca and Paula, drove up from New York. When these two hotties strutted down the dorm hallway on Friday nights they left a wake of peeping heads, whispered wows, and some serious pelvic tension. We always knew the Latinas had arrived by the sweet scintillating scents of their expensive perfumes that lingered and teased for hours.

As that fall semester wound down, Octavio made an offer I couldn't refuse; he invited me to join him in Santo Domingo for the Christmas holidays.

"Come on, Matt," he prodded. "You'll have the best time of your life."

My parents had recently divorced, and with the holidays unraveling into a clusterfuck, I immediately accepted.

After a sleepless week surviving final exams, I met Octavio in New York, where we stayed a few days waiting for the direct flight south. Almost a million Dominicans lived in Manhattan's Washington

Heights, so you could walk down Broadway for dozens of blocks and see, taste, hear, and smell nothing but Latin culture. *Holy shit,* I remember thinking, *this is America? What happened to Kansas, Dorothy?* Hundreds of bodegas — small Spanish stores — dominated the corners, all with music pounding out into the sidewalks where crowds milled about. As we made the rounds, it seemed that Octavio knew everyone — a multitude of friends and relatives kissing, hugging, and high-fiving him on every block. In many of the tightly packed apartments we visited, a glass coffee table sat in the living room, surrounded by couches and chairs. Inevitably, several neat lines of white powder would be spread out beside a half straw or a rolled-up dollar bill. Just as naturally as offering a cup of coffee, the hosts asked, "Would you like a few lines?" But we stuck with beer, rum, and weed.

After three pandemonious days of partying from one teeming tenement building to the next, Octavios's girlfriend Bianca gave us a ride to JFK Airport in her uncle's Mercedes. Though she usually visited the island at Christmas, she planned to spend the holidays applying to law schools. Gazing at her that day with her long dark thick hair, miniskirt, tight blouse, high heels, and muscular long legs, I thought that Octavio would be crazy not to marry her, which is what she wanted. The highly visible knife scars on her left arm from an adolescent gang fight added to her overall feminine mystique. Bianca had developed an unlikely fondness for me during her weekend visits to Boston. She often told me I was the nicest gringo in the entire United States and then let out her wild laugh when she admitted she had never before had an Americano for a friend.

As we said our goodbyes in front of the departing gate, Bianca took me aside.

"Matt," she said, lowering her sunglasses to expose her piercing painted eyes, "I know Octavio is going to fuck around down there, but let me tell you something. I have my people who will be watching him. If I hear that he's fucking around, you know what I'll do? I'll cut his dick off. You think I'm joking, right? But I'm not. I'll cut the fucking thing off in the middle of the night and let him bleed to death," she said, with a dramatic slashing gesture. "So you remind him of that, okay?"

"Ahhh, okay, Bianca," I mumbled, rushing off to catch Octavio and board the plane.

Five hours later we arrived in Santo Domingo, and after we made our way through the missing-limbed beggars and orphaned street kids, Octavios's cousin Enrique picked us up in an old Honda. Out on the urban highway, we got stuck in a traffic jam with a police car beside us. One of the uniformed young officers got out with a rifle in his hands and ordered us to pull off to the side. Immediately Enrique and Octavio started arguing in rapid Spanish. I gleaned that the cop had spotted me and the corrupt bastard smelled dollars. Octavio wanted to protest and resist, but the prudent Enrique argued that we should just shut up and give him a twenty. Enrique won out and we continued on, fighting our way through the smoggy gridlock.

We arrived at Enrique's family's house, which could best be described as a shack, located in a sultry, stifling shantytown in Santo Domingo. That night we had a few beers with Enrique's mother, and at midnight the two cousins and I stepped out onto the chaotic, pot-holed street. We hailed a cab, which swept us off to the Malecon, a Miami-like stretch of beaches, sea walls, restaurants, and high-rise hotels. Inside a swank club we sipped expensive drinks and immediately some glamour girls began putting moves on me. These high-end hookers assumed I had a wallet full of hundreds, but left me alone after Octavio sent them to hell.

A few couples — overweight American businessmen with petite dark Dominican girls — were out on the dance floor, the men moving awkwardly and the women seductively to the disco music. In a dim corner a group of raucous German women in their sixties frolicked and guzzled, celebrating a Decemberfest with some young Dominican studs. After a half hour of boring nonsense, I complained to my guides: "What the fuck are we doing here? Can't we go to a bar where regular people hang out?"

"Dude," said Octavio, pushing his chair back, "we took you here cause this is where the Americans go; we wanted to be good hosts, okay? Tomorrow night will be different. Let's go."

On the way back home, to quiet any further complaints about tourist glitter, my friends walked me through some nightmarish streets in Santo Domingo's most notorious slums. Ominous young *tigres* on the corners glared at my towering white presence. Crack-head street prostitutes in their underwear begged to give me a blowjob for a few dollars. As I fought off a red-eyed frazzle-haired crazy who grabbed my crotch with one hand and for my wallet with the other, Octavio cackled with glee.

"Hey gringo," he called. "You want to be down with the real people? It's pretty real here, huh?"

Back at Enrique's, with the help of more beer and battery-powered miniature fans in our faces, we slept through the humid tropical night and the sun-soaked morning, waking up in the late afternoon. After eating some rice and beans we prepared to hit the streets.

With the holiday party season in full swing, the neighborhood bars overflowed with revelers. An electric atmosphere permeated a club just a few blocks from Enrique's home. The females wore skin-tight stretch pants with colorful revealing tops, while the dudes sported Nikes, jeans, designer baseball hats and well-ironed dress shirts. The club consisted of a large open space with thin brick columns holding up a zinc roof over a massive slab of concrete. A few hundred people were packed in that night, half on the dance floor and the others sucking down beers at tables. When the Merengue band took a break, the jukebox pulsated with more Merengue.

Merengue! The rhythm that characterizes the unique Dominican identity immediately enchanted me. The Merengue has a simple, quick one-two beat, and it amazed me how the dancers' bodies, particularly their hips, aligned harmoniously with the music. Couples engaged in artistic improvisation through turning, spinning, and endless sensual moves. Both Octavio and Enrique were accomplished dancers and wasted no time. Octavio—tall, dark, and limber—stood out in the crowd with an arresting charm and a nirvanic smile. Women pushed and shoved to get a dance with him. When he led a cutie through a breathtaking choreography, I noticed an inner essence in him that I had never before perceived. The glow on his face seemed mystically attuned to the rhythm as he created magic with each of his partners. "Dude, you're in a zone," I yelled from the sidelines. He earned a deeper level of my admiration, but he also stirred up some primal envy. *Shit, how can I get into that zone?* an inner voice kept repeating.

At the bar we hooked up with two of Enrique's male cousins, and the five of us grabbed a table. I sat fascinated, slugging down cold beers in the dripping humidity. Around three o'clock in the morning, with the club about to close, negotiations that I didn't fully understand began between our table and an adjacent one filled with females. As the bar cleared out, our newly formed entourage spilled out onto the sidewalk and meandered towards the nearest pay-by-the-hour hotel. Couples began to form, and as my personal host and translator, Octavio had smoothly arranged one of the girls for me. Maybe she wasn't the prettiest or most voluptuous, but she had the sweetest smile.

Inside the hotel we paid a nominal fee for five rooms, and then came the chasing around, pillow fights, and hide-n-seek. Nothing like watching girls wrestle each other to put you in the mood. We passed around small bottles of rum as further negotiations about who was going with who continued: dating game, Santo Domingo style. Eventually we all coupled up and retreated to the privacy of our rooms, each with a dingy single bed. Not much different, I thought, from a Boston College dorm on a typical party weekend. Sweet sounds of squeaky springs, lust, and laughter rumbled through the thin walls. One couple got off on shouting out a play-by-play account of their activities for the rest of us. "Shut up," we all hollered back. Out on the sidewalk ninety minutes later, frivolous promises were made; then, with a flurry of kisses and hugs, the girls parted in one direction and we headed in the other.

After a few more similar nights, I learned that Octavio had access to just about any unattached female in these bars for the following reasons: His looks could kill, he danced like a star, and most importantly, he lived legally in the U.S. Apparently, every young Dominican senorita dreamed of escaping the island's stifling poverty and social immobility. While a marriage to someone like Octavio could provide the quickest route, most girls understood the long odds of that happening, outside of getting knocked up. But getting showered with consumer goods from a boyfriend in New York provided a promising alternative. The girls also pressed for info about Octavio's brothers, cousins, and friends in Washington Heights; any type of connection to the North offered hopes and dreams of visas, green cards, and dollars.

Given Octavio's rock star status, a constant estrogen buzz swarmed around us. For the first week I accepted a passive role in the bars as I sipped on the smooth Presidente beers, but I longed to join my amigos out on the dance floor. After throwing down at least eight cold ones on a sweltering Saturday, I found the courage to approach a seemingly shy, heavy girl. She smiled graciously, took my hand, and led me out into the gyrating crowd. I faced her, held her hand and waist, and attempted to imitate the couples around us. But since my hips were incapable of swinging from side to side, I could only jump up and down.

Unwilling or unable to follow my lead, my partner grimaced, and it hit me that something was dreadfully wrong. She violently ripped her hand from mine, screamed some vulgar expletive, and backed away. Then, in the ultimate insult, she pointed her finger at me and laughed until her eyes watered. I saw dozens more eyes staring, and then came the collective howling and screams. In a state of shock, I apparently continued jumping up and down until realizing that it was my gawky movement that had sent the crowd into an uproar of hilarity. In shame, I lowered my head, retreated to our empty corner table, and gulped two quick beers. Thank God neither Octavio nor

Enrique had witnessed the spectacle. I wallowed in a dejected state, staring at all the dancers.

Inexplicably, a bold burst of divine inspiration rescued me. Whatever it took, I decided, I'd learn the Merengue. Maybe I'd need a miracle, but I'd figure it out. I'd fallen into a pit of despair with this fiasco, but I'd claw my way back to the surface. On the way home that night, I confessed my new obsession to Octavio.

"Relax, man," he responded. "You're having no problem hooking up with women, so why bother?"

He just didn't get it. I sulked, but secretly kept on believing.

While Bachata and Reggaeton have crept and pounded their way into mainstream Dominican culture, Merengue still remains the dominant rhythm on the island. While in previous generations the elite considered the Merengue a crude representation of the vulgar campesino, the dictator Rafael Trujillo had elevated the dance to a highly respected cultural expression. In Santo Domingo it was impossible to escape the rhythm. It blared from every apartment building, supermarket, corner store, bar, club, bus, restaurant, and car that passed by. How could I forget the image of a two-year-old in a shantytown, nonchalantly swinging his tiny hips to the Merengue beat as he stood on a dirt street waiting for his mother to barter prices at a fruit stand? It seemed that without the rhythm the whole country would come to a standstill; Merengue fueled the very pulse of the Dominican existence.

You can't learn unless you are motivated says John Dewey. But while pumped with desire, I had no roadmap, no lesson plan, no instructor. A revved engine, I felt stuck in neutral; that is, until destiny kicked in. Then the universe began to conspire as the Merengue goddess heard my plea. One night at a bar we ran into two older women, longtime friends of Octavio. He hadn't seen them in years, and they greeted him like a long-lost son. Both dark-skinned and in their early fifties, they appeared much younger, with thin strong bodies and kind beaming faces that projected a deep serenity. When they grabbed Octavio and took turns with him out on the floor, I guessed that it was their love of dance that maintained their feminine charm. As activists who had spoken out and organized against political corruption, both had spent years in jail as political prisoners. Now they stood out as living icons among the political left in Santo Domingo. I appreciated that they didn't harbor resentment towards me, a Yanqui from the superpower that decades before had bulldozed their fragile democracy.

"Come by our place to visit," begged Sofia, handing Octavio her address. "Every day's a party this time of year."

The next Saturday, Octavio and I followed up. They lived in a second floor apartment with a balcony overlooking one of Santo Domingo's main streets, not far from the ocean. We decided to spend a night and then head out to visit Octavios's mother up north in Santiago. We arrived at their spacious apartment at noontime, and in two hours it was packed.

Sofia cooked feverishly and served rice, plantanos, beans, and chicken. Maria took on the role of hostess and tended a table with rum, ice, cognac, coke, and limes. Merengue rhythms vibrated out of the massive speakers in the living room. Sofia noticed me staring at several dancing couples and took my hand.

"You want to dance?" she asked.

I froze, still traumatized. "No, I can't dance," I mumbled with shame. Feeling like a coward, I wondered how I'd lost my bravado and determination.

"Of course you can," she coaxed, her thin, strong arms pulling me out on the floor. But my strong resistance caused her to pause.

"Okay, gringo," she said with a quick hug, sensing my fear. "I have to go back to cooking, but later you're going to get a Merengue lesson, okay?"

"Ahh, maybe."

Her sincerity gave me a sliver of hope that I held on to, in spite of pounding negative thoughts. Several dozen people—friends, relatives, neighbors—dropped by the apartment to gossip, drink, and dance. Children ran in packs from room to room and teenagers made out in the hallways, corners, and balcony. By midnight the guests had filtered out; the close of another day in the Christmas party marathon. Although mildly intoxicated from sipping beer for ten hours, I remained wide awake.

"So, my gringito," said Sofia, taking off her apron and pouring some rum. "You want to learn Merengue? Come with me."

"He'll never get it," yelled Octavio over the loud music.

"Thanks for the support, asshole," I retorted.

She took a gulp and led me to the center of the tiled living room, held my hands, and gently moved her hips from side to side. "Just move your hips like me," she coaxed.

I tried, but again, instead of moving from side to side, I went up and down, bending my knees. Filled with self-loathing, I clenched my jaw as demonic forces swooned in to grip and paralyze my consciousness. Octavio and Maria tried some empathetic coaching from the sofa, and Sofia continued to hold my hands. But my hips were frozen, locked. While occasionally I had "danced" in Boston clubs, rock and roll had always been about jumping up and down. My dance career had been strictly one-dimensional: vertical. As much as I loved Merengue, my body rejected any alignment with the rhythm. I couldn't shake out of my gringo disability.

After ten minutes of barren efforts, even the patient Sofia sat down on the sofa, perplexed and exasperated. As the pressure mounted, the music sounded more alien and I felt doomed to eternal hip stagnation. I stood there as stiff as a New England pine tree and watched the three Dominicans engaged in a heated discussion. Suddenly, they all fell silent and met my eyes. Sofia ceremoniously approached the liquor table and poured some Brugal, the potent local sugarcane alcohol — Dominican moonshine.

Appearing like a sorceress in her long flowing black gown, she handed me the full glass and ordered: "Drink this."

Powerless to resist, I obeyed, taking huge gulps. My throat burned, my face contorted, and my stomach felt like red-hot coals.

"Now listen to me," said Sofia, with sanctimonious authority. "Close your eyes, and when I turn up the music, keep them shut. Let the music enter your hips. Let the music tell your hips how to move. Don't think. Trust the music."

The alcohol exploded in my head, erasing fears, inhibitions, and anxieties – talk about brain chemistry! I broke into a wide grin and felt a hazy blue ecstasy ooze out through my head and take over my body. My senses heightened as time stopped; the music became my world. Miraculously, the thumping beat found an opening. Snapping out of a deep trance, I heard screaming and clapping. When I opened my eyes I saw my three friends high-fiving. I looked down, and my hips were swaying; now it all seemed so natural, so easy.

"Don't stop," screeched Maria. She took my hands and joined me. I welcomed her energy, and our hips moved as one.

"You've got it, gringo," yelled Sofia, her voice hoarse after twelve hours of cooking, rum, and chatter. "You got it, and by the grace of God you will never lose it!"

Octavio doubled over. "And I underestimated you, brother," he howled.

For the next hour I continued dancing, alternating between Maria and Sofia. I don't remember much more about that night, other than a deep sense of liberation. I was told I passed out on the living room couch and then they carried me into a bedroom.

As I lay in bed the next morning with more than a slight hangover, I remembered my victory. With a sudden jolt of fear, I rushed into the living room and put on a Merengue tape. I stood beside one of the speakers and moved my hips with ease. Praise the Lord for muscle memory! Now I had overcome my alien status. Now I could join in communion with the Dominican masses.

After breakfast Octavio started packing with haste. He had arranged for a friend to drive us north to Santiago. He confessed that he had more than one motive for the trip. In addition to visiting his mother, he had an old girlfriend there, Ana. Her husband had gone to New York for the holidays and she'd been calling.

"Ana was my first love," said Octavio with dreamy eyes, justifying his adulterous acts even before committing them. "So she will always be mine."

Bianca's hand gestures at the airport flashed through my mind, but I quickly repressed the chilling image.

As I reluctantly started to organize my suitcase, an overwhelming sense of loss engulfed me. I had known Maria and Sofia for less than twenty-four hours, but the thought of leaving them produced an acute pain in my gut. I felt like a baby being ripped away from a warm, sweet nipple.

Sofia sensed my reluctance. "Octavio," she said, "how long will you be in Santiago?"

"About a week."

"Why don't you let Matt stay here with us? That way he can continue with his Merengue."

Overcome with hope, I couldn't predict how my protective guardian would react.

"You want to stay?" he asked.

"Yeah, man, is that okay?"

"Sure. I'll see you in a week." He gave me a firm hug and ran out to catch his ride.

Maria and Sofia's calm, soothing energy permeated the apartment, making me feel welcome and comfortable. I realized these two women were a couple deeply in love and had some type of open relationship. They often had both male and female visitors sleeping over in their spacious bedroom, where three king-size mattresses were mounted side-by-side in what looked like the world's largest bed. I could only imagine the multitude of activities they engaged in behind the doors when they had a visitor, or two, or three. I assumed they found multifaceted ways to share the abundance of love in their hearts. For sure, I felt welcome to enter that intimate space, and it was tempting because both of these women oozed with sensual beauty. But I decided it best to maintain some distance and they never pressured me.

Two hours after Octavios's departure, the party started back up. A torrent of visitors arrived, and everyone drank lustily into the night. Sofia ordered every female guest to dance with me, and most obliged. An occasional rum kept my inhibitions down and allowed me to ignore my burning feet, calves, thighs, and hips. With each dance partner my rhythmic confidence grew as I learned one more step, one more turn. As long as my hips held the beat, I could increase my daring improvisations.

With the party still jumping at midnight, I polished off a final glass of rum for one last hour of hard dancing. After most guests left, I stood in the shower for about a half hour and experienced a level of exhaustion I had never known. A year before I had run the Boston Marathon—an intense four hours. But that day I had danced about ten hours straight with just a few short breaks. Luckily, I alternated between glasses of rum and water; if not, I would have collapsed from dehydration.

Even though my body ached and blisters covered my feet, a peaceful exhilaration enveloped me as I fell into the deepest sleep. At about four o'clock in the morning I awoke to use the bathroom. I lay back on my bed, smiling at the full moon shining in through the open-shuttered window. A wondrous ocean breeze cooled the tropical night and delivered a salt-tinged freshness. Feeling a giddy anticipation, like a kid on Christmas morning, I closed my eyes and floated through various levels of increasing tranquility. Then slowly I sat up, and at the foot of my bed stood a most beautiful woman.

I felt a wave of panic from her overwhelming presence, but her captivating smile put me at ease. She had dark, shining skin and long thick braids, some of which reached down her back and others adorned her shoulders and chest. Stunningly gorgeous, she wore a low-cut, flowing green dress covered by a jeweled red shawl. Sparkling diamonds surrounded her neck and fell from her ears. I inhaled a heavenly aroma and noticed the outlines of her thick nipples through the soft silk.

While I never heard her voice, somehow we communicated.

I knew I had to be dreaming, but then again I was fully conscious. She told me to honor and cherish the gift that she had bestowed upon me. She explained that the merging of body and spirit produced one of nature's great alchemies and that it would lead to a deep and fulfilling joy. With no exchange of words, a revelation penetrated and illuminated my consciousness: Sensuality is a path to the divine. As I bathed in her radiance my whole body tingled with a soothing ecstasy. She continued smiling at me and gradually faded away. Basking in the glow of the full moon, I could only laugh as I fell back in bed, hugged my pillow, and drifted into the deepest of sleeps.

The next day I awoke with a tranquil zest. I had never felt so rested, so alive, so grounded; a new warmth emanated from deep within my chest. I greeted Sofia and Maria with strong exuberant hugs, which they accepted as if the norm. After coffee, the ever-cheerful Sofia invited me to the back of the apartment.

"I hesitated to show you this, Matt," she explained. "I didn't want to scare you, but this is an important part of our lives, our spirituality."

I learned that Maria and Sofia practiced a religion known as Santeria, a popular belief system throughout the Caribbean and Brazil that synthesizes aspects of both African spiritualism and Catholicism. In this corner of their apartment they had created an elaborately decorated shrine. An altar with space for two people to kneel lay in front of artfully designed wooden shelves that were covered in white and red silk cloth against a marble background. Dozens of candles flickered beside bowls of fruit and vases filled with freshly cut flowers. All sizes and colors of beads complemented the delicately embroidered cloth. An image of Christ on the cross with Mother Mary and Mary Magdalene at his feet stood out in the altar's center. They were surrounded by at least two dozen statues of Catholic icons, including Joseph, Saint Theresa, Archangel Michael, Archangel Gabriel, and others with dark skin that I didn't recognize.

Several of the female saints wore long flowing gowns that covered their heads and bodies, but one with dark skin wore an enticing green dress and beads that flowed over her half exposed breasts. She had a flower in her long braided hair and seductive painted eyes. *What an ingenious concept,* I thought: *a sexy saint.* Then it struck me like a Caribbean hurricane. Here stood a representation of the luscious lady who had visited my bedroom just hours before. I starting shaking and broke out in a sweat. I thought of telling Sofia, but decided that instead I needed to take a walk.

I found my way to a nearby beach and walked along a massive seawall. In all my twenty years of being immersed in Catholicism, the notion of a saint of sexuality, a goddess of passionate love, had never surfaced. We had an all-powerful virgin goddess who brought me great comfort. I loved her, felt protected by her, prayed to her, and respected her above all; but why didn't we have a sensual goddess? I felt cheated. No wonder the mystical and much-rumored Mary Magdalene elicited such fascination from yearning Catholics.

Many of the nuns and priests in my Catholic grade school had satanized our sexual impulses. As budding adolescents we were ashamed of our relentless masturbating, which we were assured would lead to purgatory or outright hell. But that didn't stop us. Then in our mid- and late teens we accepted and needed sex, but it was treated as a biological necessity. In this paradigm, our budding spiritual needs conflicted with our hormonally-charged instincts and produced the most destructive of all human emotions: guilt, which the Catholic hierarchy seemed to utilize in a quest for control over their flock.

Wow, I pondered, the thought of bringing erotic sensuality into the Catholic catechism.... But given the rigidity of the Vatican, the chances of that happening were the same as the Material Girl Madonna being canonized a saint. But here on this Catholic tropical island they seemed to have figured it out — or at least they were trying to.

As I watched the Caribbean waves roll and crash, my mind continued to race. In spite of the Church's repression, particularly in relation to feminine sexuality, I had to hand it to the Jesuits. After twelve years of Catholic grade school, there I was, studying at Boston College, a bastion of Jesuit education. With their grade schools, colleges, and universities established worldwide, the Jesuits had an enormous influence and track record in education. And it was in the classrooms of this esteemed Jesuit institution in Boston that I learned about the radical feminist theology of Professor Mary Daly, the anima archetype of Carl Jung, tantric mysticism, the Goddess of Robert Graves, the Rosicrucians, the Kama Sutra, the provocative sexual theories of Wilhelm Reich, and the erotic art of the Hindus. As one of the world's proven vanguards in liberal arts education, the Jesuits seemed to be semi-clandestinely enabling us to break out of the Vatican's narrow sexual dogma.

In a euphoric state I returned to the apartment, where another day of partying was well underway. After a quick rum, I danced with a new visitor, Maggie, a beautiful, vibrant woman of thirty who happened to be Sofia's niece from the city of Bani. She had recently divorced and needed to release the tension of a stressful year. Maggie's mother had agreed to take care of her two kids so she could visit the fun-loving aunts. A single working mother, Maggie hadn't been out in months, so she was aching to party. As I danced through the day, every once in a while a barefoot Maggie graced my arms. Tall and thin, she had Octavio-like dance skills and we moved freely between Merengue and the more romantic Bachata rhythm. After recklessly throwing down a full glass of rum she kissed me on the balcony, laughing as her tongue pushed an ice cube into my mouth. At that moment I knew we'd be sleeping together. I never did find out if Sofia had arranged this hook-up or just assumed it would happen.

During our first sleepless night, we experimented with endless choreographies in bed. When Maggie rubbed and pressed her small breasts into my chest as she panted and moaned, it seemed like she desperately wanted to merge our hearts. This sweet, highly experienced woman initiated me into a new, never-imagined level of sensuality. I learned that the ultimate goal of our lovemaking was to explore and discover how close I could get to becoming her and how close she could get to becoming me. Sex became a means to achieve this ambitious and ecstatic union. Through Maggie, I received the mother of all gifts: a deeper understanding of intimacy. My mentor demonstrated to me that sex is a means to enter the world — enter the very being — of another person. And in this magical, sensual, mysterious space she led me to staggering depths of emotion that I would eventually claim and own.

Inseparable for the next three days as we drank and danced from the living room to the bedroom, we squeezed every minute out of our temporary paradise. Maggie missed her kids terribly, and they were calling on the phone every few hours. When she packed it in to leave for Bani, we cried in each other's arms and vowed to meet for a rendezvous in a year's time.

About an hour after Maggie left, Octavio strolled into the living room, giving me a huge smile and thumbs-up when he saw me still going strong on the dance floor. The next day we had to say good-bye; in five days spring semester would kick off up in Boston. Sofia and Maria made us promise to come back for the next Christmas, and they gave us a grand send-off.

"Keep dancing gringo," they laughed from the balcony as our taxi pulled away.

Julio met us at JFK Airport on Friday night and immediately we dropped off Octavio, who was crazy to find Bianca. We planned it so I would hang out with Julio on Saturday and then on Sunday we'd all take the train to Boston, ready for classes on Monday. I recounted the highlights of the trip to Julio at his aunt's house as we sipped on Budweisers. He was delighted by our adventures but not surprised.

"Hey," I asked. "How's Bianca?"

"She's fine."

"So she won't cut Octavio's dick off after all?"

"No, they'll be okay. Shit, they've been through this for almost five years now. She found out something, but she dealt with it up here."

"What do you mean?"

"Well, you know how Octavio went up to Santiago to visit his ex — what's her name, Ana?"

"Yeah."

"Well, Bianca is from Santiago, so she got word right away."

"Shit, so what happened?"

"Well, she was ready to buy a ticket to go down there and fuck them both up, but then she found a different solution. Thank God!"

"Which was?"

"She heard that Ana's husband Tomás was in New York, so she found him at a party. She seduced him that night and she banged the hell out of him for about a week. Then she kicked him to the curb like he was road kill. Poor dude had fallen in love with her and was a mess. But hey, he has his wife in Santiago to go back to. He already left."

"Does Octavio know?"

"Not yet. He will eventually though. But Octavio's not the jealous type. I think he and Bianca will be having this issue all their lives."

"Did Tomás know what Ana and Octavio were up to down in Santiago?"

"Hell no."

On the Amtrak, the three of us laughed all the way to Boston. Classes started, we got back into campus politics, and we pretty much took over the student newspaper. Octavio and Julio went back to their weekday adventures with the white Catholic girls, and Bianca and Paula visited on the weekends. They often invited me to go to one of the Latin clubs in Boston, where I continued to practice my newfound dancing skills.

One day in early March, I went with Julio to visit his cousin in the Spanish-speaking neighborhood of East Boston. Walking down Bennington Street we came across a storefront that had a display window with several dozen religious figures.

"What's this?" I asked Julio.

"Oh, a Santeria store; they pop up in the immigrant neighborhoods."

I stopped for a minute to examine the variety of saints, and in their midst, smiling brightly, there SHE was. I wanted to stay and gaze at her, but the biting wind caused Julio to grab me.

"Come on, man," he said. "I'm freezing. "

Wow, I thought, feeling her warmth radiating in my chest; *she's followed me to Boston.* I blew her a kiss and promised to return as Julio pulled me up the street.

Don't Mess with Tanya: Stories Emerging from Boston's Barrios

Discussion Guides

Mariposa

1. Describe Jazmin's personality.

2. What is your opinion of Jazmin's mother's words: *"That's what's wrong with this country. Teenagers out of control. You need a good beating, not just a slap."*

3. How would you describe the friendship between Jazmin and Jamal?

4. What do you think are the long-term psychological effects of all this violence on the kids who know the victims?

5. Jazmin refers to the cycle of violence that perpetuates gang feuds. How do you think it is possible to break these destructive cycles?

6. Do you think skipping school and going to the site of Bomba's death is a healthy way for Jazmin to mourn her loss? Explain.

7. Jazmin says that she might be a "Catholic Hindu." Do you think it is proper for people to choose elements of different religions to make sense of life?

8. What is your response to Jazmin's belief in reincarnation?

Substitute

1. Many urban public high schools in the U.S. are failing. Who is to blame for this situation and why?

2. Does Matt's description of a typical day in a contemporary urban high school seem realistic? Explain.

3. What is your opinion of the female student who snitched on Jamal?

4. Matt asks: *"Could I ever forgive Jamal without first evening the score?"* Do you think it is possible to forgive someone who has wronged you without first getting even? Explain.

5. In the story it says that Susan *"made it clear that she didn't believe that African-Americans and whites could attain a genuine intimate relationship; just too much historical baggage."* Do you agree with Susan's statement? Explain.

6. If you were Matt's supervisor at the high school and heard about Matt's threat to Jamal, would you fire him? Why or why not?

7. Matt says that *"when Susan looked at me, she saw a descendant of a slave master who had raped female slaves."* Do you think Susan is being fair to Matt? Explain.

8. If a white person and black person were to marry in today's modern society, what types of challenges would they need to overcome in the course of their lives?

9. How do you think Matt has changed from this experience? How do you think Jamal has changed from this experience?

Jealousy

1. Do you think that Fatima is a positive influence on Rosa? Explain.

2. What is your opinion of Rosa leaving her child behind in Brazil?

3. In what ways did the macho culture affect Rosa's life in Brazil?

4. What do you think are the roots of jealousy in human beings?

5. Both Rosa and Fatima are "illegal" immigrants. What is your opinion on this segment of the population in the U.S. that consists of over 12 million people?

6. Do you think jealousy affects both men and women equally? Explain.

7. Fatima and Rosa are proud of themselves for not working in strip clubs like some of their acquaintances. Given the way they deal with men, do you think they are hypocritical? Explain.

8. What do you think of Rosa's manipulation of Thiago and Bobby?

9. What is your opinion of Fatima's rhetorical statement: *"What's better: love with money, or love without money?"*

Manhood

1. List some potential consequences for Marco if his wife hadn't stopped him from getting "street justice" with the bat?

2. It says in the story that Sonia was unfazed by Marco's machismo. How would you describe machismo? For you, does the word "machismo" have a positive or negative connotation? Explain.

3. Sonia says: *"Those kids are lost. They are filled with rage and have no fear. What they do have though is guns."* Why do you think these kids were filled with rage?

4. What is your opinion of Sonia's statement: *"We can't fight hate with hate. We have to rise above them. We'll never win against them with violence?"* Is she being realistic?

5. List some pieces of advice that Willie gave Tito. Explain whether or not you agree or disagree and why.

6. Sonia says, *"I find you more a man, my love, when you use your mind, not your fists"* What do you think of Sonia's statement? Do most females think this way?

7. Write your own definition of manhood. Does running away from a street conflict fit into your definition?

Don't Mess with Tanya

1. A moral code was engrained into Tanya's being which required her to get even with anyone who wronged her. Do you think this is a positive or negative aspect of her personality? Explain.

2. In the story it said that Tanya was able *"to break barriers of race and culture with ease."* Do you think it is easy for students of different cultures and races to become friends in a large urban high school?

3. Do you think Mr. Gerrity is a realistic character? Explain.

4. If you were the Principal at Tanya's high school, would you have suspended her for her behavior with Mr. Gerrity? Explain.

5. Do you think that the issue of "minorities" getting watched or followed while retail shopping is a major problem in our society? If so, how do you think it can be addressed?

6. Do you think Tony was justified in being fearful of the young black and brown youth who walked by his store each day?

7. Do you think what Tanya did was fair? Explain.

8. Who is more of a victim in this story, Tony or Tanya? Why?

9. What is your definition of a "racist"? Is Tony a racist? Why or why not?

10. Do you think that Tony has learned a lesson? If so, what lesson has he learned?

11. Do you think it's a good idea for Tanya to go back to the store to shop? How do you think Tony will react if she does?

Mission Hill Neighbors

1. What types of advantages in life does Paul have that Cristina is lacking?

2. What is your opinion of Cristina's explanation of how she entered and stayed in the world of prostitution?

3. Should prostitution be a crime? Give reasons for both sides of the argument.

4. Why do you think that most clients in prostitution across the world tend to be men?

5. Do you think that this Christmas Eve experience has truly changed the lives of both characters? Explain.

6. Who do you think has the most difficult struggle ahead of them, Paul or Cristina?

7. What is your prediction on how Paul and Cristina will relate to each other in the future?

8. How realistic do you think this story is? Explain.

Good Hair Day

1. Briefly describe each woman's attitude towards relationships with men: Patrice, Shaniqua and Maria.

2. In your opinion, which woman is the closest to getting it right?

3. Patrice is about 15 years older than the other two women and has very different expectations for the man in her life. Do you think that women's expectations in relationships should change as their age changes?

4. Were these three women rude by ignoring Matt during their conversation? Explain your opinion.

5. Shaniqua seems to fear getting deeply involved in a relationship. Do you think she is setting herself up for a lonely life?

6. Patrice says, *"If you shoot for the ideal and expect nothing less, you are setting yourself up for a very frustrating and bitter life."* What is your opinion of this advice as it relates to relationships and life in general?

7. Do you believe that the traditional marriage is still a viable option in our modern society? Why or why not?

8. In describing her husband, Patrice says, *"his children have always been his priority – that's the sign of a real man."* In your opinion, what are the signs of a "real man"?

Love Campaign

1. Was Tanya wrong in pushing Kevin to have this relation-
    ship? Explain.

2. Given the differences in their ages, situations, and experi-
    ence, do you think Kevin should have taken the responsibil-
    ity to prevent this relationship?

3. From Tanya's point of view, what are the positive and nega-
    tive aspects of the relationship?

4. From Kevin's point of view, what are the positive and nega-
    tive aspects of the relationship?

5. What do you think was more life-changing for Tanya: the re-
    lationship, or being part of an historical political campaign?
    Explain.

6. What is your reaction to Kevin's statement that he had an
    "open relationship" with his fiancée?

7. How do you define "being in love"? Do you believe that
    Tanya and Kevin were "in love"?

8. Do you agree with the saying: "It's better to have loved and
    lost than never to have loved at all"? Explain.

Merengue !

1. Matt says that he never thought about entering Julio and Octavio's room to sit down and talk like he did with white students. What are some of the barriers that often keep individuals from different cultures and races apart.

2. Why do you think it was so important for Matt to learn the Merengue?

3. What is your opinion of Sofia's and Maria's lifestyle?

4. How would you explain Matt's dream of the "goddess"?

5. The narrator says he felt love from Maggie even though they were only together for three days? Do you think instant love is possible or was it an illusion?

6. What is your opinion of Bianca's way of dealing with Octavio's adventure with Ana?

7. What are the lessons that Matt learned on this trip? Do you think that any of these lessons will have value in his life? Explain.

8. From what you know about Bianca and Octavio, do you think their relationship has a future?

CPSIA information can be obtained at www.ICGtesting.com
233905LV00002B/153/P